THE HANDLER

THE CELLS OF KALASHOV

VI CARTER

CONTENTS

Other Books by VI Carter

MAFIA GAMES #3

MAFIA BOSS #4

<u>WILD IRISH SERIES</u>

FATHER (PREQUEL)

VICIOUS #1

RECKLESS #2

RUTHLESS #3

FEARLESS #4

HEARTLESS #5

<u>THE BOYNE CLUB</u>

DARK #1

DARKER # 2

DARKEST #3

PITCH BLACK #4

<u>THE OBSESSED DUET</u>

A DEADLY OBSESSION #1

A CRUEL CONFESSION #2

<u>BROKEN PEOPLE DUET</u>

BREAK ME #1

SAVE ME #2

WARNING

This book is a dark romance. This book contains scenes that may be triggering to some readers and should be read by those only 18 or older.

NEWSLETTER

J OIN MY NEWSLETTER AND NEVER MISS A NEW RE-
LEASE OR GIVEAWAY.
https://view.flodesk.com/pages/5f609c6c410e0d3355340e44

BLURB

BLURB

I'm The Handler for the Bratva Mafia—I tie up loose ends.

Lucca

When a ship transporting seven highly valued assets is attacked and six of them stolen, leaving behind a dead security team and one witness, I'm brought in to handle the situation.

But this isn't my usual cleanup job.

I'm an assassin, not a detective.

I'm handed a black-haired beauty who spits lies. I need to uncover the truth she's hiding in order to find the other assets.

There's only one problem—*her.*

Everything about her calls for me to take her, but she is pure, untouchable.

A highly valued asset to the mafia.

One taste of her could cost me my life.

Evie

I was ten when I was stolen.

Snatched by the sea.

Taken to a world where virgins are put on pedestals—untouchable.

Until they are sold

When six of the girls are taken and our private security team slaughtered, The Handler is called in to find them.

He's dark and dangerous.

Not a man I should trust.

But I have to trust that he can find them, and I'm willing to do anything it takes to get them back.

Once he finds them, I will make sure he sets them free, even if it costs me everything.

PROLOGUE

EVIE

I'M TEN AGAIN.

I can smell the salt that the wind carries along its long arms and dips into my hair, stirring the long strands. My lip tugs up painfully as the broken shells and small pebbles dig into my bare feet. My toes automatically curl around the pebbles to keep my footing.

I grip my hair and push it back while looking at the small light that shines in the cottage window, guiding me back to the warmth of my bed.

It's tempting.

My dad always said the water called to me like a sinking ship called to the captain. He's right. I know I shouldn't be out here this late at night, but the salt on my lips has me stepping closer to the crashing waves.

My skin tingles with the whip of the harsh breeze and the antic-ipation of the ice-cold water. I'm walking faster. The smile on my face is growing. An excited scream I can't hold in pours from my mouth and collides with the roar of the waves.

Water rushes over my feet, and I have a sense of belonging. Even at the age of ten, the water is where I am free, where I'm on an adventure. The water embraces me and bites me at the same time.

Sound shifts as a wave takes me under, and I open my eyes. Nothing makes sense, really, but I know it's the ocean. I know I'm being swallowed into a different world. My body grows weightless, and I let the ocean carry me along, the white spray of another wave rolling closer. I'd laugh if I weren't underwater. I'm spun out of control, and I give myself over to the ocean. The surface splits above my head, and I take in a lungful of air as I ride the wave back to the shore.

I'm breathless with happiness and turn to the sea again. I'm ready to take another ride. I pause. An old wooden boat, which is bigger than a rowboat, moves across the waves too fast. Even at ten, I think it's too fast. I can't see anyone in the boat but watch as the waves raise it into the air like an Olympian raising a trophy.

It's flung around as it rides up onto the shore, the impact against the stones nearly tearing it apart. The sea spits it out, and I wait until the waves recede before running along the shore to the wreck. My ten-year-old brain is excited about finding treasure inside the boat. The idea of a hidden message or even a hidden map has my small legs pumping faster.

A green tarp covers half the inside of the boat. Gripping it, I pull it back. I'm aware of the wave rising up again behind me as I pull the tarp off completely. A small body is curled up on the floor of the boat. Her legs are so white, and that's what makes the red marks on her ankles so stark. Her frame lies motionless on the bottom of the boat. I think she's my age, but I can't be sure, as her hair covers her face.

I jump in, ready to pull her out, ready to help her, when the wave that I had forgotten about covers us both. I have a split second to reach out and grab her raw wrist before we're lifted and dragged back into the sea. I know fighting with the ocean is pointless, so I try to allow it to take me.

This time, when we spin and shift, it isn't like before. I'm afraid for the girl I have in my grasp. The water keeps us under longer than it normally does. My lungs burn, and I open my eyes to the darkened sea before my head collides with something sharp. I hold her hand until I can't any longer, and I'm sinking.

I open my mouth to call out for my dad. Water pours in, and the burn in my lungs has me gripping my chest. That's my last memory of home.

CHAPTER ONE

LUCCA

"**L**UCCA, TAKE A SEAT."

The silver-haired man is not one I have had the privilege of meeting before now.

"Thank you, Igor. It's an honor." Unbuttoning my suit jacket, I sit down across from him. Behind Igor is the steel-and-glass jungle of our city. A city Igor rules with no mercy.

"This is a sensitive topic. One I want my best man on."

I reel with the compliment. Igor leans closer, placing his joined hands on the desk. A silver band with a ruby in the center is the only jewelry on his thick fingers.

I'm tempted to drag my leg up, but I remain still as Igor's small blue eyes roam across my face.

"You are good at what you do." His lips, which hang low on his face, turn up slightly as he wags a finger at me. "That job in London…" He trails off as his smile grows, and the admiration in his gaze would give the illusion that we're friends and I should relax.

An illusion—that's all this is. "Thank you."

He nods several times before his lips crumple back into their down-turned positioned on his face.

"A yacht that was transporting highly valued assets was attacked as it was docking."

I'm sitting forward now, as this is business. This is what I do. I handle situations. More precisely, I handle people. Ones that the bratva need eradicated for good. I get the call, do the job, and no one ever asks how I do it or where the person disappears to. It's a gift.

"The full security team was wiped out quickly. Camera footage, of course, is gone. All the assets were taken. I know this isn't your area, Lucca." A soft knock at the door has Igor glancing at it. "Come in."

I'm tempted to turn in my seat. I'm tempted to see the face the voice belongs to. I have a knack for faces and names.

"The Torpedo is here to see you, sir. I knew you would want to know."

The Torpedo is a contract killer for Igor. Is he putting two of us on the job? I work alone.

Igor's gaze slides to me. I haven't taken my eyes off the man. He nods at whoever is at the door before he continues speaking to me.

"Another matter, Lucca." He exhales loudly and turns to his laptop. He hits a few keys before he pauses, stares at the screen, and turns it to me.

An image of a young woman pacing a room fills the camera. She doesn't look up, so I can't see her face, but the white lace gown that hugs her body makes my trousers tighten. Long black hair flows down her back. She turns and looks up at the camera. Frightened eyes darken before she looks away and sits down.

She's beautiful.

"She is the only asset that wasn't taken," Igor says.

I haven't looked away from the screen as she sits down on the bed and drags her legs up to her chest. Her bare feet dig into the mattress.

"Why wasn't she killed?" The moment I say it, my skin grows tight across my bones at the thought of anyone destroying something so beautiful.

The screen is moved, and the image of the young woman disappears.

"She hid. That's what she told my men. She's the only witness."

A tingle races along the back of my neck, but I don't reach back and scratch it. I'm assuming the other assets were women too. The fact that they're highly valued can only mean one thing—they must be virgins. They make a lot of money on the black market.

"I need you to find out what she saw and get my assets back."

Igor moves papers around his desk.

"No disrespect, sir, but this isn't my area."

Igor looks up at me. "I know that. That's why I want you on the case. You have always shown great discretion, and you get every job done."

I sit forward. "Assassinating people," I remind Igor. That's my job, my role in the Bratva. I'm not a detective.

Igor's lips drag up. "You will get to assassinate people, no doubt about that, Lucca."

Irritation makes my skin tight.

"I want you on this."

I can't refuse. I've already spoken out of place.

Igor picks up the phone and presses only two buttons. He's ringing someone within the building. "Bring her in here." He hangs up.

Igor pushes documents over to me. "All the information about the layout of the yacht, codes…" He waves a hand in the air as the door opens behind me.

Footsteps are heavy—a male. There's a second set that is cushioned, and I think of the barefooted woman. I don't turn but take the papers off the desk as a large security man steps to the side.

She appears a second later. Her blue eyes shine with fear. Tears have left marks on her creamy skin.

Igor stands and walks to her, takes her hand, and presses a quick kiss to it.

"My beautiful Evie, everything will be okay."

This is very personal to Igor. The fact he knows the beauty by her name makes me pay even more attention. A small blue diamond mark on the side of her thumb clarifies my suspicions about the girls. They are virgins. The marking is a brand that men with lots of money know. Men who could pay millions for someone like Evie.

"This is Lucca, and he will be taking care of you."

For the first time, Evie looks at me. Her collarbones jut out sharply as the air is dragged into her lungs. Fear lights up her blue eyes.

"He will help us." Igor takes her chin in his thick fingers, dragging her gaze away from me. "You need to help him, *printsessa.*"

She doesn't answer, and Igor releases her before sitting back down.

I want to keep looking at Evie, but I know better and focus on Igor, who has returned to his laptop.

"Any information you find out, you can update me here." He turns away from the laptop and copies a number down from the screen onto a small piece of paper, which I take from his outstretched fingers.

I put the piece of paper into my jacket pocket. This whole situation isn't standard, but once again, I remember my place and don't question Igor. Circling in the back of my mind is that I've been set up to fail.

I rise as Igor walks around the desk. He pauses at Evie. "Don't disappoint me."

His words have her nodding.

He takes my outstretched hand and pulls it to his abdomen. His gaze meets mine. He doesn't have to say the words. They're shining in his eyes. I'm not to disappoint him either. He releases me. For Evie, her sentence might be a brothel, but for me, it would be death.

The large security man leads Evie outside, and I follow. My eyes can't help but take in the curve of her ass. She glances at me over her shoulder as if sensing me watching her. She's quick to look away as I bypass her. My own security men rise as I step into the lobby. All three fix their headsets and adjust their suit jackets.

They fall into step around Evie and me as we leave the lobby and step into the elevator. Only then does Igor's security veer off. My gaze searches the lobby for The Torpedo, but he's nowhere in sight.

The ride down is long from the top floor of the building. Evie's shoulders are hunched; a small rise of them lets me know the beauty is breathing. She's terrified, and that's not always a bad thing. I need her more than she can imagine.

The doors open, and we file out, my men flanking us as we leave the building and enter the waiting limo. Evie and two of my security join me in the back. Michail rides up front with the driver.

The limo shifts as it moves into a lane of traffic. She's leaning toward the blacked-out windows, staring at the steel world as it moves by slowly.

"What did you see?" I ask her.

She sits back, like my voice startled her. Blue eyes flash from me to my security. I could tell her no one will hurt her, but that's a lie. One dead girl and the rest saved would be better than no girls for Igor. I will do what I need to in order to complete this task. No matter how strongly her beauty draws me in.

Even as I think of hurting her, my skin grows tight again, and I open my suit jacket. Her eyes dart to my fingers before bouncing back up to my face.

"There were men." Her accent is unusual, a mixture of Russian and something else that is sharp. She swallows and toys with her hands in her lap.

"Lots of men." Her gaze is fixated on her hands, and when I don't speak, she looks up at me. Her gaze glazes over. "They were so quick. Like ghosts."

"How many?" I keep my tone sharp so it pierces through her foggy memory.

Fear is curling up her thoughts tightly. I've seen the look in so many eyes, the same look she's giving me now.

Pain often pierces it, but right now, I'll try with my tone.

Her brows drag down, and she scrunches up her face before relaxing it again. "Five, six…" Her lips move like she wants to throw out more numbers, but when she looks at me, she slams them shut.

"What did these men do?"

Lenny, who's to my right, is leaning slightly toward Evie, hanging on her every word—or hanging on her beauty.

"Anything you want to add, Lenny?"

Lenny snaps back in his seat. "No, boss."

I haven't looked away from Evie, but she's glancing at all three of us. "They… they killed all our security." Now she won't look at me at all, and her lack of sharing piques my interest. She's hiding something.

"All the security were in one place?" I ask.

Her head snaps up to me. "There was an incident on the boat." Her fear is gone, a defensive tone taking over.

She doesn't expand on what the incident was, and I don't push; instead, she squirms, and when the limo stops, Pavel opens the door.

"After you," I say to Evie.

She gathers the white material around her and climbs out, giving me a nice view of the curve of her ass. I follow, and Lenny moves behind me.

The ride up to the penthouse is quiet. Evie places herself close to the doors, and I don't mind standing at the back and taking her in. A body like hers, never having been touched, is a fucking temptation. The doors open, and she steps out into the penthouse.

My men go to their usual spots. Lenny stays by the door, Michail moves into the main room, and Pavel starts a search of the house. I can hear the radio in Lenny's ear buzzing with the word *clear* as Pavel checks each room.

Evie doesn't move. I remove my jacket and hand it to Lenny before pulling off my tie.

"All clear." Pavel returns to the room moments later, and I'm released from my spot at the doors. I have too many enemies, so I can never be too careful.

"Sit down." I point at the large L-shaped couch that takes up a portion of the main room. Evie moves toward it and sits on the edge while staring straight ahead. Now that I have her in one of my homes, I'll continue my questions.

"The incident that attracted all the security, what was it?"

Her shoulders stiffen at my question.

I pour myself a small vodka and walk over to the couch. I don't sit down. Instead, I stand across from her, leaning on the fireplace, which I don't think has ever been lit.

"One of the girls wasn't well."

The lie falls from her lips, and once again, I'm fascinated with her accent. I can't place the mix. Her bottom lip is larger than the top, both chewed from all her distress.

"Is that normal that the whole security team would attend to one sick girl?"

She tightens her hands in her lap again. I can see the nervous tremble that takes over her fingers. No matter how tightly she holds them in her lap, I see them shake. "No." Her one word is a whispered lie.

I empty the glass of vodka. "Why don't you get some rest."

Her blue eyes widen, and she's nodding in agreement like it's the best idea ever. She rises, and I step closer to her. "The rest might clear your head and stop all the lies from pouring from your lips."

She's shaking her head, color pouring into her creamy skin.

I take another step closer, and instead of her fear growing, her eyes harden, and she juts out her chin and holds her head higher.

"Do you know what they do to pretty liars?"

Some of her defiance shrivels away. She's smart enough not to deny she's lying, but I still don't like how defiantly she's staring at me.

I take another step. I don't touch her, but I'm close enough that if I wanted to, I could. "Girls like you can make a lot of money from one buyer. But it's not the only option. Have you heard of the mill?"

She holds up a shaking hand with the small blue diamond tattoo.

I laugh, and she flinches.

"Oh, printsessa." She flinches again at the endearment that Igor had used for her. It means Russian Princess. "That little diamond won't save you."

I step away from her terrified stare. "Get some rest and clear your head," I say over my shoulder. Lenny holds out my jacket, and I take it.

"You want me to go with you, boss?" It's Michail who asks.

He's always the one I take, but not today. I can't seem to forget how Lenny stared at Evie in the limo. It shouldn't bother me, but it does.

"You stay here. I'll take Lenny."

Lenny covers up his surprise quickly and follows me into the elevator. I tug on my suit jacket, and as I look up, Evie is still staring at me with horror shining in her big blue eyes. I don't blink until the doors close, cutting me off from the beauty.

I'm going to the boat. I need to see what happened for myself and try to understand why Evie is lying.

CHAPTER TWO

EVIE

I don't move long after Lucca leaves.

The space around me sways and dissolves until I'm back in the loading bay.

I was curled up as small as possible, my heart beating faster than the wings of a trapped butterfly. Leah, one of the girls, always caught them in a glass and enjoyed watching them trying to escape when it wasn't possible. She said that was us—beautiful butterflies in glass cages.

I never showed my irritation toward her; instead, I would wait until she got bored watching the butterfly panic and flap and would leave the room. Once she was gone, I would lift the glass and set the butterfly free. It would soar to the ceiling, looking for a way out. The windows had bars on them, but I could open it enough to allow the butterfly its freedom.

I knew I would be free one day, too. Releasing them gave me hope. Releasing them made me feel I had power over something in my life.

My stomach tightens as I think about how that turned out. Hiding behind all the crates, fearing the security could hear my heartbeat thrash in my chest.

My name had been repeated, barked, and I knew if they found me, my disobedience wouldn't go unpunished. It wouldn't be a slap on my wrist.

My shoulder aches again, a wound long healed, but it's a different kind of pain. I think they call it phantom pain. Like when someone loses a leg, initially they still think it's there, they still want to scratch an itch, they still want to stretch out a muscle or just wiggle their toes.

My wound still burns and throbs with its own deeply rooted phantom pain.

I slowly come back to Lucca's living space, and I'm ready to reach back and touch the old wound on my shoulder, but I don't.

I glance to the left, where one of his security watches me. I raise my chin higher, trying to hide the pure fear that wants my frame to crumble and bend in two.

"I'd like to be shown my sleeping quarters." I speak as clearly as possible.

He doesn't smile or give any indication that he heard me, that is, until he moves. His footsteps are extremely quiet on the marble flooring. I expected the solid black shoes to make a tapping noise, but they're are soundless, like my bare feet.

I gather the dress higher, not wanting to trip, and all my training about walking with grace comes flowing back into my mind without my permission. It's in me, like a path laid in my brain. I fear I'll never dismantle it. Maybe I could build a fresh path alongside it one day, but I can never remove it. I just know it. Like I know it's air that fills my lungs.

The security man pushes a door open but doesn't enter. He pushes a small black device into his ear.

"Pavel. I'm taking her to the third guest room. Do you want to cover the door?" He stands and waits for a reply, nods at the large white wooden door before standing aside.

I enter, not surprised that someone will watch the door. I don't close it. It wasn't something we were ever allowed.

Pavel's footsteps are heavy, and I listen to the rhythm as he makes his way down the hallway. He arrives at the door and gives me a once-over with disinterest in his brown eyes before facing forward.

The door remains open as I turn to the guest room. It's large, but I'm used to large. I'm used to luxury, and this is luxury.

My heart stutters and stalls in my chest, and I cover it with my hand, not wanting it to grow frantic. It's Leah's screams. They were the loudest. I open the wardrobe; it's empty apart from towels, linens, and a dressing gown.

Closing the doors, I take my time and move around the room. A smile that shouldn't be possible crosses my lips, and I bite my lip to stop it. I have no right to smile. But on the head of the four-poster bed is a carving of a mermaid ready to jump into the waves that rise up to greet her.

I want to touch the waves. Even brown and wooden, there is a beauty to whoever carved them, and I'm moving until the tips of my fingers touch the cold wood. I tilt my head and close my eyes, trying to remember the feel of the water on my fingers, but it doesn't come rushing back like I hoped it would.

My eyes snap open, and I'm moving toward a large arched space. There are no doors, but plants act as a concealment as I step into a bathroom that's as large as the bedroom. A tub you can step down into becomes my sole focus.

We never had the luxury of our own wash space. Someone did that for us. Different faces, half-covered with red material, would arrive twice a week, and we would be bathed in the same room.

My hands fumble with the taps, and ice-cold water sprays out. The shock of the cold water has a scream falling from my lips that's so close to a laugh.

Pavel's heavy footfalls have me looking at the archway as he steps into the bathroom.

He doesn't ask me what I'm doing, fully clothed in a bathtub. He presses the black device in his ear.

"All clear," he says before turning and leaving me. The water is freezing as I kneel down and hold my hands under it. A tremble starts quickly, but it jump-starts memories I have craved for far too long.

I'm screaming as something large splits the water behind me. Panic, glee, and something I can't explain has my small chest pumping as I focus on the shore ahead of me. Large, strong arms wrap around my waist, and I'm airborne.

"I got you." My dad's voice is muffled as he pretends to eat my stomach. He got me every time we played this game. He was the shark and me, the victim.

His face fades, and I push my arms under the cold water, trying to revive it, but his face disappears. Tears of joy and pain make a pathway down my cheeks as I hunker over and try to force my foggy brain to bring my dad back to me, but it's too distant.

I can still see the freckles on his arms, along with the silver bracelet with a Celtic design he wore on his right wrist and never took off. I'm shaking from the cold water, I'm shaking from what just happened, and I'm shaking from my past.

I turn off the taps and sit in the cold tub until I have no choice but to get out. Standing, the white dress is heavy. Reaching back, it's a struggle to open the buttons, but I manage to get them open. The heavy material pools around my feet, and I climb the three steps out of the tub. A full-length gold mirror covers a third of the far wall.

I'm not the girl I see in my head. I'm not a girl. Time has frozen for me inside, but on the outside, I'm a woman who's fully developed. I separate my long black hair and bring it forward to cover my large breasts. The white panties leave nothing to the imagination as I step quickly across the room and pick up a towel. I wrap it tightly around my body.

My body is a temple. I'm a goddess that will be adored and cherished. That was the teaching. We learned about different men, some attractive, some not so much. But we had to learn their names, likes, dislikes. If they selected us, we had to know about them.

Some girls left our group very early on, and fresh girls replaced them. But most of us grew up together.

Lucca wasn't one of the men we learned about. I would never forget someone like him. My cheeks burn as I leave the bathroom.

I can picture the girls' reactions if Lucca was one of the selected. I'm sure he would cause quite the stir. Opening the wardrobe, I take out a nightdress and wrap it around my body. Once I'm covered up, I let the towel fall to the floor.

I spot a pair of feminine white feathered slippers at the bottom of the wardrobe. I'm ready to slip them on but pause. I love the freedom of not wearing shoes. We always had to wear soft slippers. No hard skin would ever be allowed to develop on our feet.

I close the wardrobe door, and a sense of elation has my stomach squirming. I'm looking at the door, expecting to see one of the girls, expecting them to tell on me, but it's just the back of Pavel's head.

The room grows smaller, robbing me of my earlier reprieve.

"May I explore the penthouse?"

Pavel turns to me, his soft brown eyes not really belonging to the hard set of his jaw. A contradiction that leaves me unsure if I should relax or accuse him of his deceitful eyes.

"She wants to 'explore' the penthouse." He emphasizes the word explore. His gaze never leaves me as he speaks to the other security member on the end of the mic.

He steps aside. "Go ahead."

I hold my head high as I pass him. I pause at the door and decide to take a left. The hallway isn't very wide, and the lighting is low. I'm not alone. Pavel's clunky shoes give him away as he follows a few paces behind me. I open each door but don't enter the rooms. Three bedrooms, a gym, then two locked doors have me circling back toward my room. I don't enter but keep walking until I'm back in the large open space. Windows that run floor to ceiling flood the space with light. I don't go over to see the city below. Heights aren't something I like.

I continue walking into a kitchen area; that's where the other security man is. His eyes aren't soft. The blue in them is washed out like he's seen too much from life. He has that same hard set of his jaw that Pavel displays.

I keep walking, opening more doors, including a study that doesn't look like it's been used. Then two storage rooms, two more locked doors, and a master bathroom I do step into. Large white statues of lions are placed on either side of the entry. The room is tiled black and white, and it takes me a moment to realize the whole room is a wet room. Several showerheads hang overhead, their golden heads like large-sized plates. Walls of red brick are placed around the space, with lots of plants on them. I can only imagine this room flooded in water.

"Yeah, okay."

I half turn toward Pavel's voice.

"I'll be back in a minute," he says and leaves the room.

I listen to his footsteps, and I'm moving to the door as he disappears around the corner, and it's the first time no one is watching me.

I'm blinking, my mind screaming for me to run, but I calm the storm inside me. That kind of panic will get me nowhere. I need to learn, and fast. I'm moving, remembering the study. Saliva pools in my mouth as I think about what I'm going to do.

I pause at the study door before entering. Pavel's footsteps are distant as I slip into the room. There on the table is a phone—an actual phone. I close the door and listen for Pavel, but there's nothing. The floor under my feet seems to grow further away as I walk to the phone. I'm sure it's a mirage, but as I touch the device, my heart soars.

Picking it up, I'm slow at bringing it to my ear, expecting to hear a dead tone, but it's live.

My fingers move across the number pad, my heart filling my throat. A disconnected number has me swallowing more saliva.

No.

I dial my home number again and again until my heart truly feels like it will shatter on the floor.

No.

Eight years. It has been eight years since I disappeared from the shore of County Clare.

Eight years since I saw my home. Eight years, and now, I was forgotten.

CHAPTER THREE

LUCCA

I'm met by security at the docked boat. They must have been stationed here.

They don't ask me who I am. They already know. A gate is open, and I walk from the platform onto the ship.

"Has anything been removed?" I ask the security who follows me in.

"No, we were told not to touch anything. That everything had to be left for you to see first."

Good.

Another set of security is just at the entrance as I enter the ship.

"I want to see the security room." That's my first request.

"This way."

I'm led down a wide hallway. The inside of the ship is luxurious. Nothing is out of place. The floor we walk down is clean. I duck my head as we enter a large security room. Seven stations circle the room, each one with several screens.

The security moves ahead of me.

"This one watches the *resursy* quarters."

I sit down in the chair. "You know they are human?" I ask as I turn on the screens that have darkened.

"We must always refer to them as assets."

I glance back at him over my shoulder. "What's your name?"

"Sacha, sir." He stands taller.

"Okay, Sacha. You know how to operate all this?"

He nods, and I get out of the chair.

Each camera blinks to life. Bedrooms, a large sitting room. Each room is empty.

"This stream is fed to one place." Sacha gets up and taps at a large black box in the center of the room. "It all goes here. Backup is in the lower decks. Both of them were wiped."

Someone did their homework.

"Take me to the girls' rooms."

I follow Sacha, and it's a maze. You would have to either have a map or be familiar with the layout.

"I want a roster of everyone who worked here in the last six months. I don't care if they scrubbed a toilet or steered the boat."

Sacha nods. "That's already in the process of being prepared for you."

The room we enter is large, and it's one I've seen on the cameras.

"Which one is Evie's?" I'm looking at all the beds, waiting for Sacha to point her space out to me.

"We didn't know their names. So I don't know."

I'm looking at Sacha now. "How long have you worked on the ship?"

"Three years." His answer is swift.

"And you never saw which bed the girls got into."

"This is the first time I've ever stood in this room. Only women were allowed."

They really didn't want anyone to defile these women. I move around the room, but there are no trinkets. Every girl seems to have the same space, the same items. There's nothing to suggest any individual qualities.

I go through all the girls' rooms but find nothing.

"One of the girls was sick. Do you know which one?" I ask.

"I can find out," Sacha says as we re-enter the hall.

"Take me to the loading dock."

Sacha's face hardens at the mention of the loading dock, and I'm assuming I'm in for a treat.

I am.

Ten bodies are scattered around the space. Small pools of blood have gathered around their heads and shoulders from the large gaping wounds across their throats.

I scan over all the bodies. The slice is clean. Whoever did it was left-handed. The cut starts shorter on the left side and deepens into the right.

"No footage from this space?" I ask, already knowing it's gone. But I still ask.

"None. Everything throughout the ship was wiped," Sacha informs me from the door.

Each kill is the exact same. Someone who was fast and silent. Or maybe there were several of them.

I bend down and look for any more markings on the bodies, but the only wound is the slice across their throats. This security man's face is covered in acne. I move to the next and notice a small red dot just along his jawline. It might be nothing, but as I continue to check, I see it on all men.

"When are they being sent for autopsies?"

Sacha's laugh is quick and short as I look at him. "They aren't. Their throats were slit."

I rise and look around the floor. I'm not sure what I'm looking for, but I don't find anything. "I want a full autopsy performed," I say and glance at him.

He nods. "Okay."

He doesn't sound convinced, but I'm not here to convince him. I'm here to find out who did this, and from the looks of it, the security wasn't at full capacity. The small red mark could be a tranquilizer. Maybe.

"What's in the crates?" I ask, pointing at the large stack of them.

"Food," Sacha answers.

I walk over to the first one and try to pry it open, but I can't with my small penknife.

"Can you open one?"

Sacha gives me the same look he just gave me a moment ago when I suggested that the bodies needed to be autopsied. He goes to a small station and reappears with a crowbar. I stand back as he pries the crate open. Once it's open, I lean in.

Sacha doesn't say anything about the stacks of cocaine inside the crates, but as I glance at him, I can see the surprise in his eyes. I cut open the bag and taste it.

It's cocaine, just like I thought.

"I'll need the log for the loading dock for the last six months too." I'm not sure if any of this is linked or if the men were told it was food so they wouldn't go near it, but either way, I need to do a thorough check.

I stay another thirty minutes going through the ship, but nothing is out of the ordinary. Sacha promises to get all the paperwork back to my penthouse within a few days.

★★★

"Pavel is watching her," Michail informs me the moment I step into the penthouse.

I remove my jacket and think of how best to approach her. She isn't forthcoming with information about what happened, and I want the reason why that is.

I rest my suit jacket on the arm of the couch before I make my way down the hall. Pavel greets me at the open door, and I don't pause but step into one of the guest bedrooms. There's no sign of Evie.

The plants on either side of the archway into the bathroom have me tilting my head to try to see her. I pause as I step into the bathroom. She's standing across from a large golden mirror, looking at herself. Her large breasts are perky. The pink nipples have my cock hardening against my trousers.

Breasts that have never been touched by a man. The longer I stare at them, the harder my cock grows.

My gaze trails down across creamy skin, a flat stomach, and all the way to the white beaded panties that cover her pussy. Light reflects off the beads, and she looks like a goddess.

The panties don't cover her ass; it's just a string that's sucked up between perfect round cheeks I'd love to spank. Her long legs are perfect—a nightgown pools around her feet.

My gaze travels right back up to her face. I take my time since she doesn't know I'm looking. Then her gaze clashes with mine. Her eyes grow round, but she doesn't move. I take a step deeper into the room.

Her gaze darts down to my trousers, where my hard-on bulges; I don't try to hide it. Color pours into her creamy cheeks like molten lava.

I take another step, and her nipples harden. She's turned on, too.

"You shouldn't be looking at me." She holds her head high as she speaks. Her accent has me clenching my jaw. Everything about Evie just wants me to fuck her. Would I pay a million bucks to have her? It doesn't seem such an outrageous price now that I'm standing in front of her. Her beauty is almost otherworldly.

"Why not?" I ask and purposely let my eyes roam across her flesh.

She doesn't move or reach for her dressing gown. She doesn't try to cover up her body.

"Only my future husband is allowed to look at me."

I stop at her tone. "You don't like the idea of that?"

She flinches like I called her out on something, then bends to gather up her robe. Her long black hair falls away from her shoulders, revealing a scar.

"I thought you had to be flawless."

My words have her snapping up straight. She drags the dressing gown over her flesh and cuts me off from looking at her any longer. But now that I know what lies under her clothes, I can't erase that from my mind. I don't want to.

"We do." She pulls her long hair out of the back of the dressing gown before fastening it.

"It doesn't look like a birthmark." I walk right up to Evie, and she doesn't so much as blink. She also doesn't stop me as I drag down the dressing gown just enough so I can examine the scar on her shoulder. My thumb brushes across the puckered flesh, and her sharp inhale has me looking up at her.

"This is a burn mark."

Her steady gaze never falters. "It is."

I run my thumb across it again, and her inhale of breath isn't as sharp, but I still hear it.

"It's from when I first arrived." Her accent is getting thicker, telling me she's upset.

I want to ask where she arrived from, but I don't interrupt her.

"I wasn't compliant." Her lip tugs up, giving me a flash of perfect white teeth. This close, I'd expect to see a blemish on her skin, but she reminds me of a china doll. Flawless except for the one mark. I run my thumb across it one more time before stepping back.

She pulls the dressing gown back up. "It was a lesson I learned the hard way."

I can still see the defiance in her gaze. The same she displayed toward me. But now that I'm really looking, I think it's more toward this situation and not just me.

The idea of someone branding or burning her makes my gut tighten.

"This is why I haven't been selected." She raises her chin again—a defense mechanism. "You're flawless in every other way. It's hard to think one small piece of flesh would do damage."

"You don't know the men we're being sold to. They don't like any flaws. Hard skin, even bad skin, would turn them off. A burn…" She tightens the belt of her dressing gown.

"It's odd that they would mark you, then. Devalue you."

Her gaze snaps up to me. "Well, they did." Her words are harsh, and I feel there's so much more to this story than she's telling me, but I drop it. I step closer to her until we're shoulder to shoulder. She turns her head to face me, her heightened breath fanning across my face.

"You're beautiful, Evie."

Her cheeks flame again.

"But something about you doesn't quite fit right. It's like the equation is off-kilter."

She presses her lips together like she can keep all her words deep inside her.

I grin at her. "I like a challenge. I'll get my truth." I step away from her and let my words sink in. Being around her, especially after seeing her naked, is hard.

Too hard.

Michail is in the kitchen area.

"What did she do while I was gone?" I don't like the idea of any of them seeing her naked.

"She wanted to be taken to a guest room. So I took her, and Pavel guarded the door."

I open a bottle of sparkling water and fill a glass.

"She wanted a look around, so we allowed it. Pavel was with her."

I take out two painkillers and wash them down with water. "At all times?" I ask. It's a standard question, but when Michail pauses, I turn to him.

He swallows. "No. There would have been a brief time she was alone. Forty seconds to a minute."

A lot can happen in that time frame. I'm not fucking happy. I leave the kitchen area and walk back to Pavel. The green light on his headpiece blinks. Michail sent him a warning.

"What took you away from your one duty?" I ask.

"Michail needed me." Pavel looks nervous, and I don't want to squeeze the truth out of him. "There was a naked woman in the other building."

"You left the only witness we have to help us solve this case so you could look at pussy?"

"It was a minute." Pavel's voice lowers.

He's been with me for years. I step away, and when he tries to defend his stupidity, I raise a hand.

I walk away from Pavel and don't even look at Michail. I hear a low curse. Yeah, they know they have fucked up. The study door is slightly open. I push it open fully, and the phone and laptop on the desk have me ready to step back out and hurt Pavel.

I pick up the receiver and redial the last number. It gives me an automatic no longer in service message.

She tried to ring someone.

I leave the study. "She tried to ring someone," I tell Pavel.

He pales. "It was a minute."

"Get the fuck out of my sight."

Pavel is quick to move.

"Michail," I call.

He appears. "Guard the door until I find out who she called."

"Boss—"

I cut off his words before I end up cutting off his fucking head for his incompetence.

CHAPTER FOUR

EVIE

I HAVEN'T LEFT THE bathroom. Something heavy dropped into my stomach when Lucca called me out on my lie. Now all I feel is the cold of his words.

He called me beautiful. That thought pressed heat against the cold inside me. It was something I've been called my whole life. It just felt different from his lips. The girls called me beautiful. Every lady who took care of us called me beautiful. The words from his lips… felt different. It felt like a stamp of approval, which is ridiculous because so is he, just in a different kind of way. His beauty is all the sharp angles of his strong jawline. His deep silver gaze, which when zoned in on me, sends shivers racing across my flesh like an army of small ants.

His beauty is sharp, dark, and alluring.

Dangerous.

I step away from the mirror with the thought of how he looked at me. I've never desired to be touched. Some of the girls touched each other. I didn't think it was wrong, but it never interested me. It was a part of me I refused to explore. I had lost my freedom for it. I'm still losing my freedom for something we were taught to put on a high pedestal. On one hand, I value it because it kept me out of being sent to the brothel like some girls were. On examination, we got our markings. A black tick on the wrist was the one every young girl dreaded.

Yet, I want to get rid of my purity so I have no value to them. It's a silly thought that has me releasing air quickly from my lungs. I would have other uses. We all do.

My mind is damaged, and somewhere in the recesses sat my sanity and understanding of the depth of what I had been brought into.

A shiver snakes across my skin, and I can't pull the dressing gown any tighter across my flesh to try to shield it off. I start to leave the bathroom but pause over the threshold at the sound of Lucca's voice.

He's right outside my open bedroom door. "Guard the door until I find out who she called." His words are growled.

I'm moving but gather myself at the last second and pause before barging after him. The muscles around my heart squeeze painfully, and I clutch my neck like I can stop the fear and panic that are erasing all logical thoughts from my mind.

My legs start to move as fear clouds my judgment. The one called Michail glares at me. He's ready to ask me something, but Lucca's voice fills the hallway.

"Don't speak to her."

Dread curls its bony hands around my stomach, and all I can think of is what have I done?

If he traces the number to my home, would he kill my parents? My feet hit the floor hard. I've always been obedient. I've always had such control but never before was my parents' existence threatened.

I'm in the hallway, and Michail reaches to stop me.

"Leave her."

My head snaps up. Lucca stands outside the study. There's a knowing glint in his gaze as he watches me. "You can either tell me who you rang, or I can find out myself."

The hallway dims, and the world falls out from beneath me, but somehow I manage to stay standing. "The authorities."

Lucca claps his hands. The noise bounces around the hall. The clap is too severe. His anger pours into his fingers, and I'm tempted to take a step back.

"Final time, Evie."

Fear crawls up my spine and settles on my shoulders, weighing me down.

"A friend."

Lucca reaches me. "What a beautiful liar you are." His hand moves quicker than I could anticipate and envelops my face. "Now you have me really curious." He pushes my head back, straining my neck. "I will make a phone call of my own. I shall ring Igor and tell him what a disappointment you have been."

It's like a syringe has been injected into my skin and has sucked all the blood and life out of me.

Lucca releases my face. I want to rub the aching skin, but I don't dare move a muscle. He's waiting for an answer. He's waiting and not leaving to make that phone call to Igor. That says a lot and gives me a second to calm the sheer loss of control of my mind.

He's calling my bluff.

I force my head high like I carry all the confidence in the world. "A friend. But their number is not in service. So the phone call was pointless."

"Nothing, Evie, is pointless. Tell me about this friend."

I'm thrown off guard at his question.

"A childhood friend, and it doesn't matter. Like I said, the number was invalid."

There's a beat when Lucca does nothing. A slow tug of his lip has ice-cold fingers prodding my spine.

"I'll tell you if it matters. Do you know what I do, beautiful Evie?" Lucca juts his chin at Michail, who steps back and away from us.

"Work for Igor." I blink before glancing at Michail; why did he have to step back? Is Lucca going to punish me? I'm ready to remind him he can't touch me, that Igor would be mad, but the dangerous glint in Lucca's gaze keeps me silent.

"I'm The Handler."

My core grows hollow, as though everything inside me has been removed, all my organs, and I'm filled right up with ice-cold air.

The Handler.

The Bratva's assassin. Of course I knew who he was. I just didn't know what he looked like or that his name was Lucca.

The Bratva's personal assassin. My mind keeps circling around this fact. Why was I placed in his care? Why is he on this case?

"Do you know what The Handler does?" he asks.

I nod. Words have failed me. I could beg and plead, but I don't think to a man like Lucca that would change the outcome of this situation.

"So you know what I'm capable of." He takes a step closer until his cologne surrounds me. It's a stark reminder that I haven't been around men much, especially not ones like Lucca.

The Handler.

"Please." It's silly. It's pointless. It's naïve, but I have to try.

His grin of delight is frightening. "Who did you ring?"

"A friend."

"Stay in your room." His departing words have a chill sliding over me. Michail reappears, and I step back into the room, knowing for the first time I've really messed up. Before, it was my life on the line. I knew that from the moment I hid behind those crates in the loading bay. Now, it's my parents.

I can't stay here and just wait. I have to escape. I have to find a way home. I have to warn them.

The thought of returning to the shores of County Clare sends too many emotions crashing through me like a storm, orchestrating waves against the rocks.

I stay in my room, and the door remains open. I often hear Pavel's footsteps; he's the only one who seems to move around. Michail leaves my door when the third security guard takes his place. Time passes in a blur, and fear keeps squeezing me until I'm mentally exhausted.

It's Pavel, with his soft brown eyes, who brings me food. I eat it all. I taste nothing and have to force each swallow down. I make sure nothing is left on the plate.

I'm surprised when clothes arrive. Pavel once again is the one who brings them in.

He doesn't speak but lays all the bags on the bed and leaves. I check through the bags of colors and find the darkest outfit. Pants aren't something I was given the privilege to wear. Dresses were all we wore. I don't think as I take out fresh undergarments. I don't think about who picked the black lacy material out but put them on before I slip each leg into tight black pants. I've done this before. Before they took my life from me.

I don't allow myself to go back. I need to stay focused. I need to warn my family. Next, I find a dark shirt. It has small white dots, but it is the best out of the sea of blue and purple that was bought for me.

I take out a pair of shoes that have the smallest heel and leave them to the side. I'll wait until I'm leaving before putting them on. I don't find a jacket, so I place the bags on the floor, lining them up in front of the wardrobe. I go back to listening to footsteps and anything that can be useful.

No one speaks. There's a static that buzzes in and out between the headsets I've seen the men wear, but that's it.

More food is offered, and it's Pavel who brings it to me.

He lays the tray down on a bedside table.

"Thank you," I whisper, and give him a soft smile. "You're very kind."

He pauses and looks at me. He's unsure, and I let my smile grow wider while half-closing my lids. I'm the image of innocence. It's a look we learned to master.

"Do you want anything else?"

It works. "No, thank you. This is great." I let my lids flutter closed, and Pavel leaves with hesitation in his steps. Once he's gone, I start to eat. Michail looks at me, and I don't think any amount of fluttering eyelids would make him bend, but Pavel has a softness I'll take advantage of.

I push aside The Handler's and Igor's faces. I'm dancing with the devil, and I already understand what it feels like to get burned.

I roll my shoulder like I can feel the lick of flames. I hadn't lied to Lucca when I told him I had been disobedient. It just wasn't something that should have happened. Veronika was the woman's name. She didn't like that I refused to strip and bathe. Being ten and terrified out of my wits didn't ease her harshness—that and the language barrier had me disorientated and terrified.

The food churns in my stomach, and I stand up and wash it down with the glass of milk. I can do this.

"I'm going to the bathroom," I speak to Michail's back. He doesn't respond, but I know he's heard me.

I go into the bathroom and relieve myself before I start my search. I find nothing useful. I'm not a fighter, but I feel I need something for when I leave here tonight. There will be fewer guards, and all I can hope for is that Pavel was the one who either volunteered or was left behind.

I listen for his clunky shoes, but I don't hear anything. I return to the bedroom and sit and wait for the night to come.

CHAPTER FIVE

LUCCA

I've sent the men home, and all I have to do now is wait. She isn't asleep. I check my watch. It's two in the morning. She's moved around the room a few times, even ventured out into the hall. I've left a hall light on so she can see, but not enough that she can see me.

I'm sitting on the couch in the corner of the room, shrouded in darkness, and like anything, give a man enough rope, and he'll hang himself. Evie doesn't disappoint as she tiptoes down the hall. She pauses in the main room and stays frozen for a few minutes. It's impressive how she molds herself into the darkness. Closing my eyes, my hearing amplifies, and her shallow, harsh breaths tell me where she is.

I want to stand up and ask her what she's doing. But the chase is more alluring. The elevator doors slide open, and I open my eyes as light floods the hallway. Evie steps in, her finger pressing the buttons repeatedly like she might be able to get the door closed faster than it's operating.

I gather my suit jacket off the couch and arm myself as I make my way to the elevator. I don't have to press anything; it automatically comes back up. When the doors open, I step into the empty metal box.

The lobby downstairs is empty. She's moving faster than I anticipated. Leaving the building, I look left and right through the sheets of rain that fall with one purpose only—to drench anyone stupid enough to step into it.

Movement across from the building has me pausing. She has no jacket, and the light shirt she's wearing clings to her body. She runs and ducks from one shop awning to the next. Stepping out into the rain, there isn't much I can do to fend it off. I stay on the opposite side of the road and watch her race from one awning to another.

She's soaked within minutes, and she's completely oblivious that she's being watched. She isn't street smart. The idea that she thinks she got away that easily is flabbergasting.

She keeps to the same pace. A couple who moves past her, huddled under an umbrella, has me pausing. Will she ask them for help?

I might have to kill them both. They don't slow down or even notice Evie. How could they not notice her? Even soaking wet, she's still a rare beauty. The moment they pass her, she shoots out from under the awning and starts running, changing her earlier movements.

I don't jog but walk faster. The moment she turns a corner, I start to run, and when she's back in my line of sight, I slow back down. We've cleared a few blocks when she finally stops. She looks over her shoulder, but I'm already in the shadows. Hope widens her eyes, and she's running across the street.

There is no way she saw me, yet she's nearly upon me. The moment she steps closer, I'll grab her and end this escapade of hers. She moves past me and pulls open the door of a phone booth. She has to kick it a few times to get it closed behind her. I know she has no money. She doesn't pick up the receiver, but she stares at it long enough that I'm ready to step out of the shadows. She picks up the phone directory and flicks through it. Once she finds what she's looking for, she tears a page out and folds it several times before stuffing it into her back pocket.

I brush more rain off my face as she puts the phone book back and stares at the phone. She finally reaches out and lifts the receiver. She doesn't touch the keypad but leans her head against the glass. Her shoulders shake.

She jerks upright and slams the receiver down. The distress on her face is evident as she turns and leaves the phone booth and starts to walk into the rain. Her hand keeps patting her jeans pocket as if she's trying to make sure the piece of paper is still there. She stops at the end of the road, ready to cross, but I've had enough.

I step up beside her.

Her shoulders stiffen before her gaze travels up to my face. Any color that had tainted her cheeks vanishes. Two guys are ready to cross the street, and before she can do anything, I pull Evie to the side and press her against a shop front.

"Don't draw attention, or I'll kill them," I whisper and press closer to her body. She smells of rain and something sweet. My lips linger close to her ear, her body is pressed against mine, and it feels fucking good to have her this close.

She's shaking under me, and when I press a kiss just below her earlobe, she freezes. The men have moved past. I know I can let her go, but I don't. I press another kiss to her jawline, and she pulls away from me, ending my kisses. I have no fucking idea why I'm doing this.

I step away and grip her hand. She doesn't fight me as we walk in the downpour back to the penthouse. The moment we enter the lobby, I see our reflection in the elevator doors. We are both soaked. Evie's gaze is on me, and I see the fear take over before she tries to pull away from my hand. The doors open, and the ding has her short-lived rebellion stopping. I pull her in and don't release her hand.

She doesn't start to plead or explain herself, and I don't ask. The more I think about what could have happened to her being on the streets alone, the angrier I become at her.

I release her hand, not wanting to crush her delicate fingers. The moment we reach the penthouse, she's out of the elevator like a bull let loose from a pen.

"Come back now, Evie!" My warning has her stalling. I remove my suit jacket, and it plops loudly on the ground beside me.

She spins and faces me; her chest rises and falls rapidly.

"Give me the paper."

Her lips drag down, and she doesn't move for a moment. She raises her chin, and I know she's going to lie. I pull off my tie and let it fall to the floor.

"I don't have anything."

Her lies have the darkness that is always there rising in me. I open my shirt one button at a time. She's trying to keep her gaze on my face, but her eyes drift lower with each button I open.

"It's sad, really." I peel off the shirt and watch color enter her cheeks. "You forget who I am."

The shirt hits the ground, and I kick off my shoes. She doesn't answer, but her lip trembles slightly as I walk toward her.

"Take off your clothes, Evie."

She blinks like the words are hard to process. "You aren't allowed to touch me." She speaks with her head high, like that will remind me who she is. She needs a reminder of who I am.

I grip the blouse on both sides and tear it open. She screams and tries to pull the material back together, but it's tattered.

"I said take your clothes off."

Real fear enters her blue eyes, and she tugs off the damaged shirt with trembling fingers. Once it hits the floor, she looks up at me but doesn't touch her trousers.

Her defiance isn't something I admire right now. She screams as I pick her up and carry her down the hallway.

She doesn't strike me or demand I put her down. She's like a rag doll across my shoulder as I open my bedroom door and throw her onto the bed. She's moving, scrambling away from me. As she turns, I grab her by the waist and drag her body back to mine.

Her heart beats wildly in her chest, her breathing erratic. I place one arm across her chest to keep her still and use the other to open her trousers. She thrashes, and when I tighten my arm across her chest, she stops.

I raise my arm to release her and drag her trousers down her legs. She starts to crawl off the bed.

Grabbing her ankles, I drag her back and climb further onto the bed.

"No! Please. I'm sorry." Her pleading should make me pause, but she's disobeyed me too many times.

My hand comes down heavily on her perfect ass, cutting off her pleas. She's frozen as I bring my hand down again; her soft, plump flesh turns red under the assault of my hand. I don't stop but strike her a few more times until she's shaking under me. Her cries have me completely stopping. My handprints on her ass have me dipping my head and pressing a kiss to her skin.

"You need to understand that I have all the power here, printsessa. And when I ask a question, I expect an answer."

She continues to cry, and I kiss the red skin.

"What were you doing in the phone booth?" I ask and spin her around. Her eyes are red and swollen from her tears. But her hard nipples press against the flimsy material of her bra.

Anger tightens her lips together, and I admire her. She's protecting someone—someone who is very dear to her. Is it a friend like she had said? Male?

That thought has my gaze roaming down her flat stomach to the black lacy material that covers her pussy.

"Are you going to answer me?" I ask as I slip my fingers under the dark material.

Her gasp has me looking back at her face, and she shifts.

"I'd advise you not to move, or I'll spank you again."

She's rooted to the spot, and I let my finger slide over her swollen bud. She gasps again at the contact, her gaze pinned to the ceiling. I should stop, but I can't.

I slip my fingers lower until two of them press along her entrance. I want to slide my fingers inside her, but I also don't want to tarnish her for when she's handed back to Igor. I slide my fingers back up and rub her clit.

She tries to move again, her focus returning to me.

"I'll gladly spank you again." I almost want her to move, and when she doesn't, I continue my assault on her clit.

Her hands clench the sheets under her. She's fighting off the sensation, and I move my fingers quicker. My cock presses painfully against my trousers, and the thought of fucking her sweet, pure pussy have me spreading her further and running three fingers across the swollen bud.

She gasps again and is ready to move away from me when she arches her back and moans. I want to taste it. I want to taste her juices, but I keep moving my fingers, thinking about how I'm the first man to make this beauty come.

She comes seconds later, her fingers tightening around the sheets, and she cries out. She continues to vibrate and shake under my hand in the aftermath of her orgasm. She's staring at me like I just appeared, and when I remove my fingers from her panties, I place them in my mouth and taste some of the sweet nectar that I'm sure still flows from her.

"You shouldn't touch me." Panic claws at her, and she's pushing herself up, but I slowly push her back down and climb on top of her, pressing my hard cock against her pussy.

"I can do what I want to you, Evie." I grip her wrists and drag her arms above her head. She smells fucking delicious. "I could fuck you right here on this bed, and no one would do a thing about it."

Her breath brushes my neck as I lean in and press a kiss to her jawline. "I'd sink my cock into your virgin pussy. It wouldn't be nice, Evie." I let a laugh slip from my lips. "It would be very nice for me." I lean out to look her in the eyes. "But not you. I'm sure you know a woman's first time is painful."

A lone tear slips from the corner of her eye, and I'm ready to stop torturing her.

"Who are you trying to ring?" I ask again and push my cock, which throbs painfully in my trousers, against her core. I want her to defy me. I want an excuse to allow my darker side to take over.

Would Igor demand the money, or would he punish me for my disobedience?

"Lucca." My name from her trembling lips has me tightening my hands around her wrist, but I pause.

More tears leak from the corner of her blue eyes. I haven't seen many women cry, not ones under me anyway. Any woman under me is normally moaning out my name, not shedding fucking tears.

I release her wrists, but she doesn't move, and her cries don't stop.

"I lost everything at ten." Babbled words fall from her lips.

I don't blink as her confession fills me. Why should I care? She's here to help me solve this case.

"I can't lose any more." Her lip continues to tremble.

"Why are you telling me this?" Does she expect me to care?

My words have her tears drying up and her sniveling stopping, but that haunted look I've seen in the eyes of too many boys digs deep and manages to worm its way beyond my rib cage. It's like a kick to my black heart.

"I don't know." She tries to curl away from me, but the weight of my body prevents her escape.

Grabbing her wrists, I pin them back above her head.

"I don't care what you lost or what you will lose. All I know is that you're here to help me solve this case. Then when I find the other girls, I will return you all to Igor." I push down on her wrists like my words can be driven deep into her skull.

I release her and get off. "Go to your room."

She stumbles from the bed but pauses and gathers her clothes. Her cries linger behind her for far too fucking long.

CHAPTER SIX

EVIE

There is this type of pain in my stomach I've never experienced before. I manage to get the piece of paper out of my jeans pocket. It's soaked, and I unfold it carefully. I'm searching for a radiator to place it on.

My mind is foggy from Lucca's touch, from Lucca's harsh words, from my own outbursts. My gaze blurs, and the room tilts. I have to pause and close my eyes and try to find my center again. When I open my eyes, I feel more like myself.

I find a hairdryer tucked away in one of the drawers and use it to dry the page.

In my eagerness to ring home, I forgot to add the prefix that allows me to ring another country. It hit me last night that If I found a phone book, I could ring home and maybe someone would answer.

I'm staring at the page as I continue to dry it. I don't need it anymore, I realize. That number will be forever branded into my memory. I turn off the hairdryer and take the piece of paper into the bathroom. I'm surprised he let me keep it. I'm surprised he let me leave that room.

His threat of having me elated me and caused a ripple of fear throughout my system. I'm trying not to think about his hands on me as I crumple up the page and drop it into the toilet. I flush and watch it disappear.

He touched me, and I didn't want him to stop. There were moments where my brain kicked in, and I half tried to leave, but his touch gave me release from the situation. His silver eyes spoke of arousal, and his own pressed so heavily against me.

Even when he was threatening to take me fully, with his groin pressed against me, fear should have been all I felt, but I couldn't deny the attraction I felt toward Lucca.

His body was defined perfectly—the outline of his muscles like gorges in the landscape.

I flush the toilet one more final time before leaving the bathroom and making my way into the bedroom, where I put on dry clothes. I find the darkest ones, which are gray. The skirt is very dark, but it touches the floor, and the top has a small red-and-yellow beaded design along the arms.

It's pretty, but not as pretty as what I have grown up accustomed to.

I hate the thought that settles in my mind. I might have gotten the full number for my parents' home, but I could never risk ringing them now. I could never risk Lucca tracing their number. He still might. My only hope is that he forgets about it.

I fall asleep on top of the covers after a few hours of twisting and turning. When I wake, it's odd not to hear the girls' chatter or feel the heat from the sun that always shone directly on my lower calves. I sit up and take in my surroundings. I'm in The Handler's home. Something tells me he doesn't live here full-time, because there's nothing personal in the penthouse, and it just has the feel of a hotel.

I get off the bed and go to the bathroom. Each time I think of last night, my buttocks clench at the memory of each slap. The pain had frozen me for a moment. But it was the heat of his hand, the feel of skin on mine, that made a completely different reaction in my body. Embarrassment had torn through me by the thought of being spanked turning me on. My mind wanders a little further to how he touched me, how I wanted him to touch me.

I wash my face and pause. There's something different. When I look up and meet Lucca's gaze in the mirror, my heart stalls, and a half scream lodges itself in my throat. My heart picks up a new beat that's wild and unwilling to slow.

"Breakfast is ready."

The silver shirt that covers his wide shoulders is nearly the same color as his unusual eyes.

I hold my head high, hoping he can't see how flustered I am. "Thank you."

He doesn't leave, and my stomach hollows out the longer he's looking at me. I can't hold his gaze, so I look away and place the towel back on the rack. When I look around, I'm alone again.

Breakfast is fresh fruit and cereal. He's set the breakfast up at the breakfast bar. Straight away, all I can think about is how unladylike it is to climb up on a high stool. I have to lift the gray skirt to get up. Lucca is already seated and doesn't hide the fact that he's watching me.

He eats his cereal slowly. Once I'm up, I feel slightly accomplished and pour out some cereal before adding strawberries and honey. Without asking, Lucca pours me orange juice.

"Thank you." I pick up the glass and take a drink.

He doesn't speak through breakfast but eats while looking at his phone. For the first time, I wonder about him. How did he end up as The Handler? Does he have a family? Does he ever get sick of it? Does he have a girlfriend? The last thought has my face flaming because I don't like the idea of him having a girlfriend. If he does, I highly doubt he would spank her as he did to me last night.

Silver eyes cut across to me, and I immediately look away. We finish eating in silence, and once we're done, Lucca tells me to get some footwear on because we're going out.

On the way down in the elevator, I attempt to ask him three times where we're going, but fear clogs my throat. Is he returning me to Igor? What would Igor do to me?

I can't stay quiet any longer once we're in the limo.

"Where are we going?"

Lucca once again is on his device. "To the ship." He doesn't look up at me as he answers.

A new wave of fear and a longing for what has become of my home has me looking out the window as I try to move all the parts inside me around like I can make them fall into place.

I can't.

Home. Home was a boat, home was a large house, home was a cell in the lower deck of a ship once. Home was County Clare.

That final thought has me squeezing my eyes from the burn in the back of my throat.

"Did you always want to be The Handler?" I need a distraction from my morbid thoughts. I don't look at Lucca because I don't really think he will answer.

"Yes."

Now he has my attention. He's staring at me, and my stomach squirms.

Him answering me is a surprise, and now I want to know it all. But I also remember that I need to be very careful with my questions.

"Why?" I wanted to ask what his parents thought of their son being The Handler, but maybe they were high up in the mafia, that this was a role he had always known he would fill, so therefore he always wanted it.

His silver eyes narrow slightly. "I just did, Evie."

My name on his lips has me wanting to squirm. It's too personal, and his gaze drags down my front like he can see through the material. Like he can see my nipples hardening in my bra. I fold my arms across my chest, and the grin on his face has me uncrossing them. The limo slows as we approach the ship. I don't know any of the security here. They're all new. As we board the ship, I feel the press of the ghosts, and my legs refuse to move any further.

Lucca was walking ahead of me and stops. "Take me to your room."

His voice snaps me out of my frozen state, and I walk up to him. His cologne is strong as I pass him and lead him to not just my room but all of our room. We always shared a space. The moment I enter it, the smells of warm sun, lotions, and perfume surround me.

I miss them all. The thought that they could be hurt or worse has me walking to my bed. The light streams in, cutting across the silken cream covers of my bed. I touch the stream of light, yet the heat doesn't penetrate my flesh like it once did. I still feel cold. As I glance around the room, I know each inch of it, but it's like I'm looking at the life of someone else—of some poor girl who has no idea what really lies ahead. Most days, I tried to pretend this was it. That I lived with a group of women, and that's how it would always be. It was an easier fate to accept than the knowledge that I was in a holding cell waiting to be sold.

"Is that where you slept?" Lucca drags me away from my thoughts. I almost forgot why I'm here.

"Yes."

He steps up to my bed and opens a small cupboard beside it. I don't stop him as he removes files. He dumps the stack on my bed and takes the first one off the pile. His gaze flickers between me and the file of one of the men who might become my husband.

"What is this?"

"It's a profile on my future husband."

Lucca's jaw tightens, and he holds a look of disbelief.

"We have to learn about them in case we are picked."

He shuffles the pile on the bed. "There must be forty here."

"Thirty-eight," I correct.

He closes the file and throws it onto my bed. He's leaving the room, but I don't like the mess. I quickly put the files back in my cupboard and follow him from the room.

"Let's go to the loading dock."

I knew this would happen, yet it still doesn't stop my heart from hammering in my chest and the blood from roaring in my ears. I walk, and once I round the corner to the loading dock, I'm expecting to see all the bodies on the floor. All the bodies I had to step across to get out of here.

"I asked about the girl who was sick," Lucca says.

The blood still taints the floor, and my stomach somersaults.

"There was none, Evie. So you lied to me."

My gaze jumps to the crates. "I was the one who was sick." I could never tell him I was trying to escape. Even admitting I was in here wasn't something I told Igor, but he knew I was lying about everything.

"Why come in here?" He's closer to me, but I don't turn to look at him.

I shrug. "I just ended up in here."

"Close your eyes." Lucca is right behind me, and my eyelids flutter closed at his command.

"What did you see?"

I open my eyes. I don't want to go back there. His warm large hand rests on my shoulder. "I'm here with you."

I close my eyes. I was behind the crates, lying in wait, as I knew we were docking soon. I had overheard the security talking about dropping off the crates, and I knew this was my chance—my only chance at getting out.

I figured getting into a crate would be the best thing to do. Only that day, I couldn't get it open, so I lay behind them as the room filled up with security.

"The guards all stood in the center of the room," I say. "I remember them creating a circle, all looking around, bewildered. Then three men appeared, dressed in black; even their faces were covered. They stepped out from the shadows."

I hadn't known they were there. I wasn't sure if they knew I was either. I doubt it, or they would have taken me, too.

Lucca's hand squeezes my shoulder.

"They had these darts—black darts with red-feathered heads. They shot them at the security. I think they drugged them." I open my eyes and look down at all the pools of dried blood. "They staggered but kept the circle." My hands start to tremble, and I need to see it's Lucca behind me. I turn, and his hand slips from my shoulder. "They had long swords, and it was quick, so quick."

Lucca nods. "Through all this, they didn't see you?"

I hold my head high. "No, I was getting sick behind a crate. I waited until they left. Found my way back to my room, and that's where they found me."

"What about the girls?"

Leah's screams pierce me now. "I don't know. I heard Leah screaming, and when I got back to the room, they were gone. All of them." And I did nothing but pray I wasn't caught.

Lucca doesn't stay any longer but leads me off the ship. He's mulling over all I've told him and is quiet in the limo. For me, I have this growing sensation like something bad is going to happen.

"Your relationship with Igor? What is it?"

"I've only met him three times. He's our keeper."

Lucca's watching me intently.

"Each group of girls has a keeper who's responsible for our safety. I often heard the security talking about keeping us safe, or they would have to answer to Igor."

"Does Igor know you were on the loading dock?"

The other shoe drops, and I understand the bad sensation that's been spinning around in my stomach.

I shake my head. "I was in too much shock when he questioned me. I didn't mean…" I trail off. "I didn't lie," I quickly say. "I just…" My lie's not helping me. Lucca doesn't react to anything I'm saying, and I have no idea what that means for me.

We arrive back at the penthouse, and I take a look up at the large building and let out a heavy breath. I was tired of men and the power they held over us. The door is opened, and I get out. The moment we step into the penthouse, I stop. Two men are waiting for Lucca. One I've never seen before, the other I know. Sacha. He works on the boat. He traps me with a look that Lucca doesn't seem to notice as he removes his jacket and hands it to Pavel.

"I hope you have some good news for me." Lucca steps into the living space, and Sacha releases my gaze.

I don't leave. No one asks me to.

"Autopsy report." Sacha hands the file to Lucca, but he keeps snatching quick glances my way.

"Interesting. Blood loss." Lucca snaps the file shut, and even I know there's something wrong. A shift in his stance. "Their blood was clean."

"If that's what the report says." Sacha hands over more files. "The roster and also the loading dock inventory."

"Thank you." Lucca takes them and quickly looks over the files.

Leah's screams assault me, but the longer Sacha and I look at each other, the clearer that memory is becoming. He was on the ship that day. It was only the back of his head I saw; he was moving through the hallways. He didn't see me. But I saw him.

CHAPTER SEVEN

LUCCA

After Sacha leaves, Evie tries to scramble out of the room.

"Stay where you are."

Her shoulders tense, but she has the sense not to leave.

All her lies, all these lies… I tighten my grip on the files before I throw them down on the couch.

The impact isn't loud, but Evie flinches.

"You looked afraid when you saw Sacha."

Evie had been chewing her lip and now stops and shakes her head.

She's afraid. I can see it. She's also lying.

"The conversation you had with Igor, what exactly was it?" I ask her and step closer.

"I told you, I was in shock."

"Try to remember, Evie," I bark, stepping closer and clapping my hands once. Making her understand that she needs to focus.

Her eyes fall to the floor. She won't look at me, and I stop walking. Irritation tightens my fists.

"If you don't help me, I will never find those girls." The moment Evie notices my clenched fists, I unclench them. "Right now, they could be raped."

Denial has her shaking her head.

"Someone could be beating them. Torturing your sisters. I know what I would be doing." I allow my gaze to drag across her frame.

Her jaw tightens, but her bottom lip still drags down.

"Or…" I open my hands wide. "They could be dead somewhere, and that would be on you."

Her eyes widen and glaze over; she's shaking her head repeatedly. I can see her folding. I'm close to breaking her.

"You are preventing me from closing this case because you keep lying to me. So what did you tell Igor?" I ask.

She wavers before her hands dangle at her sides in defeat. I hate breaking her down like that or placing those images in her head, but she needs to start helping me.

"That I was sick in the bathroom, and when I returned to my room, everyone was gone, but I heard Leah screaming." She blinks, and tears fall. Her shoulders are raised high like she can protect herself from the fear that's closing in and clouding her blue eyes.

"Okay." She's telling the truth to me now, and that means she lied to Igor. I understand the fear I see growing in her gaze.

"So what were you really doing in the loading bay?" Was she there to draw the security away from their stations around the boat? Was she part of this? Her fear seemed legit, but her want to find the girls she grew up with was questionable.

She closes her eyes, and more tears fall. Her hands are curled into small fists.

Pavel is watching her like he wants to hug her. His eyes are filling with pity, and I want to strike him and tell him to man up.

He notices I'm staring at him, and some of the pity flees from his gaze, but not enough to satisfy me.

"Go do something useful," I bark at him, and he leaves. Evie's eyes snap open at my raised voice.

"I was trying to escape. I thought I could hide in one of the crates, but I couldn't get it open."

"That was stupid of you." I'm moving closer. The anger at how close she would have come to death fuels my veins and propels me toward her. "You would never have gotten out of there unnoticed."

"I had to try." Each word is said with pain. "You must understand that. I was trapped."

I had grown up in confinement, in a camp that trained us to be the best we could be. Most boys there didn't want it. We all started at the age of six—most of us kids. I'd seen so many piss their trousers or call out for their mothers. I was glad to be trained by the best. I wanted to be an assassin. I wanted this life. That's what made me the best. We were beaten when we didn't perform up to their standards, but that's what turned boys into men. Soon, the thumps were welcomed to see exactly what your body could tolerate.

The thought of Evie being beaten leaves a whole different feeling in the pit of my stomach.

"Why? Were they hurting you?" I ask. It shouldn't matter. I shouldn't be asking, but I need to know.

She flinches in confusion, and her brows drag down over her blue eyes. "No, but I didn't belong there. They took me from my home." Her lip trembles, and I don't like how her words are making me feel.

She looks ready to burst out of her skin, and I move closer and click my fingers three times in front of her face. Her gaze focuses on my fingers. She steps backward at each harsh click.

"Stay focused," I bark. "So you were hiding in the loading bay, then what?"

"One of the security was in there. I think just doing a routine check. His radio buzzed, and it was Sacha calling all security to the loading dock."

"Are you absolutely sure?" I ask, but I already know she's telling me the truth.

"Yes. He sent them there, and they all died."

Evie appears exhausted at the confession. I can't understand why I was being lied to or what Sacha could gain from this. Was it the girls?

"Did Sacha see you at all?"

She looks away from me and bites her lip while shaking her head. "No. But I saw him in the hallway. He called my name. He was looking for me."

I'm being set up. Now the only person I can get information from just left the building.

"What are you going to do?" Evie's words drag my attention back to her.

"Are you going to tell Igor?" Fear stretches her neck, the pull visible along her creamy skin.

I ignore her and turn to Michail, who has remained quiet the whole time, but I know he's taking in every word, along with Pavel.

"This information never leaves this room." I speak over my shoulder. My men are loyal, but this was way over my head. I had no idea how high up the deceit went. Igor couldn't be involved. He wouldn't risk his neck like that. I don't think he would anyway.

I turn to Michail. "None of it."

"Yes, boss."

"Yes, boss," Pavel echoes.

"Find out where Sacha is," I tell Pavel, and he leaves at my request. I turn back to Evie, who watches me.

"Are you going to tell Igor?" she repeats.

I have no intention of telling Igor the truth. That isn't required of me. The only job I have is to find the girls and return them. That's all I would focus on. I push aside the fact that I'd hate to see anyone hurt Evie. I don't even know her, but something about her calls to the beast inside me not to hurt her but to protect her.

"I don't know," I lie. "You could have made this a lot easier if you hadn't lied so much."

"You have no idea what happens to us." She's moving closer to me like we can share this moment.

It's a dangerous thing for her to think, and I need to end it now. I grin at her, making her stop. "Once again, you have this notion that I care."

Hurt flickers across her beautiful face. She looks up in Michail's direction, and color enters her cheeks. She's not just naïve sexually, but there's such an innocence about how the world works in her eyes that it makes me care when I really shouldn't.

She grows silent for a moment. "Can I go to my room?"

I don't want her to be alone, but I also don't want to be around her much longer. She's forcing me to see her as more than a means to an end. An end that will come, and then what?

"Yes, go ahead."

She leaves, and I watch her until she disappears into her room. I wait a beat more before I turn to Michail. "How long was Sacha here?"

"Five minutes max."

"Did he ask any questions?" I enter the kitchen area and pour myself a drink. The vodka doesn't help the unsettling feeling coursing through me. It's one thing to give me a target. I would watch them, learn their movements, and remove them when least expected. That's what I do. It could take me hours, days, or even weeks, but I never got impatient. This situation is making me unsettled.

"Yeah, he wanted to know if Evie was here."

I nod. Of course he did. He must be afraid she saw something. I reopen the roster and go through the names. He isn't on it. He had a part in all this, and I want to know exactly what it was. I have two more drinks before I return to the couch and go through the remaining files. The loading inventory is mundane and, once again, a fabrication of what the ship was really transporting.

I have no idea how much of the roster is true, apart from the fact there were ten security men dead. They were the only ones that I could say with certainty were on the ship that day. The rest I had to disqualify. As for the autopsy, Evie saw the darts, she said they were drugged, and I believe her. Each one had a prick mark on their necks.

I lay the fabricated files down beside me and finish my drink.

Pavel is quick to find out Sacha's home address and forward it on to me. That's where Sacha is now. He left my home and went straight to his own, which is perfect for me.

Leaving Evie makes me feel uneasy, but Michail won't disappoint me again, and I've left him personally responsible for her. He knows if anything happens, I'll have his head for it.

I don't take the limo but my own personal vehicle. She hums to life, and I love the feel of the Astin Martin as I pull out of the underground car parking. I only use her for jobs, and she brings back a feeling I always have of contentment, and also, it's a reminder of the purpose I have.

Going to Sacha's will allow me to flex old muscles that feel abandoned.

I arrive at the address Pavel gave me. The house is like cubes stacked on top of each other. It's all glass and steel. To some, it would be stylish. To me, it looks more like a cold box.

I get out of my car, which I've parked on the opposite side of the road. Most gates have cameras on them, and I don't want Sacha to know it's me. Keeping my head down, I jog across the road. The moment I reach the gate, I take my gun out. The overhead cameras have been shot out, the glass cracked, and no lights are blinking.

The gates are still sealed, but I scale the low wall easily and land in the front garden. I see three more cameras all shot out.

Fuck.

I move to the partially open front door, then push it fully open with my foot and wait a moment. There's no sound, and I enter with my gun raised. The inside is as cold as the outside. Gray slates under my feet meet gray walls that I move alongside. There's no furniture to obstruct my movements. I round the corner and come face-to-face with Sacha. He's in a large armchair, his throat sliced from ear to ear. His white shirt is coated in a river of red. Whoever did this is most likely gone, but I do a sweep of the house to make sure I'm alone.

I am.

I check Sacha's pockets for his phone, but it's already gone. He has no wallet on him either. I check the side of his face for a red lump like I saw on the other security men, but there isn't one there. They didn't have to drug him to kill him. The fact his throat is slit tells me the same people who are keeping him silent are the ones that attacked the ship.

Movement out the back window catches my attention. The back lawn is scattered with trees, but among them, I see a flash of black. I withdraw my gun and move slowly to the back sliding door. The beauty of new homes means everything is soundless. The sliding door opens seamlessly, and I step out onto the manicured lawn. The black silhouette still hasn't moved any further away. Four trees separate us, and I move quickly until I am at the opposite side of the tree he leans against.

"Target is down, but I think The Handler has arrived. Copy." His words are deep in his throat, and I reach around and squeeze his esophagus before moving around the tree. I don't let him go as the air is cut off from his lungs. His shock slowly wears off, and I bring the butt of the gun down on his head. Releasing him, he slides to the ground. I take the piece out of his ear.

I can hear someone breathing on the other side.

"Dima?"

"Dima?"

I listen to the background noise to see if I can hear others, but it's just the one voice.

The line goes dead, and I glance down at Dima before I leave him lying on the ground and move silently from one tree to the next. I need to make sure that no one else is here.

No one else is here, but they will come soon. Whoever he was talking to would send men, especially now that they know it's me. I return to Dima and drag him up off the ground before slinging him over my shoulder and carrying him to the wall.

I could slip inside and open the gates, but instead, I fling him over the small wall. He hits the ground hard, and a groan has me hopping the wall and picking him back up.

He fits into the trunk, and I slam it shut. I should check the cameras, but time is running out, and I hope to get some information out of this guy. That's what I do, after all.

Leaving the cube house behind, I dial the penthouse—the phone rings. No one answers. I know something is wrong. I dial Michail's private number, and it continues to ring. I ring both of them again, but still no answer.

Fuck.

Pushing my foot down on the peddle, I race back to the penthouse. I shouldn't have left her. Not after her telling me that she recognized Sacha and he was a part of this. He must have made a final phone call saying she was with me before they killed him off. Whoever took all the other girls was tying up any loose ends.

I park in the underground basement and leave Dima in the trunk. He's awake, banging loudly on the trunk. If I don't shut him up, he'll draw attention. I open the trunk; he's ready to leap out. I slam my fist into his face several times, and he curls up to protect himself. But I don't stop until his body stills. His chest still rises and falls, but I hope he stays silent for a while.

The ride up to the penthouse takes far longer than it ever has. I don't take out my gun, but it's ready for when I need it. Instead, I open the control box and disable the elevator once I arrive at the top floor. Whoever is here won't be leaving. With that thought, the doors open.

CHAPTER EIGHT

EVIE

I'm back in my room, and I don't know if I feel relief or fear of telling Lucca the truth. It could cost me my life, but he's right, I am stopping them from finding the girls. If the roles were reversed, they would do anything to help get me back. His words left horrible images in my mind that I can't shake.

Images of them shackled like we were when they first took us—the day that destroyed me.

They fished me out of the water along with the girl who had tried to flee from them. The one I tried to save, but instead, they got both of us. I was one of five girls. I think we were all in shock as they dragged the girl up onto the deck. Later, I discovered her name was Helena. They made an example out of her. She died in front of us as a reminder that fleeing wasn't an option.

I replaced her on that ship. I always have those moments of looking back at my home and seeing the small candle flicker in the window. I should have turned around. I should have gone back to bed. My life would have been mine. I wrap my arms around my waist as I think of my mother's hugs.

"I miss you so much." I speak the words out loud, and they are ready to break me when Michail enters the room. He closes the door and locks it behind him. I'm up and backing away from him. He's holding his neck, and that's when I notice a dart hanging from it.

"Hide," he mumbles, and he sounds drunk. I'm back there again, back at the loading bay as all the security stumbled around.

The gun hangs from the tips of Michail's fingers, and I race to him as the bedroom door shakes from something heavy on the other side. I take the gun. It's far heavier than I expected it to be, but I manage to hold it steady as the door crashes in. My finger is held above the trigger like I'd imagine it should be.

I recognize the man straight away. He's another security member from the ship. I don't know his name, but I'd seen him around the ship a few times.

The sword in his hand is like a Samurai sword. The way he holds it tells me he knows exactly what he's doing. The light catches the sharp edge of the sword.

Michail is mumbling, but I can't understand a word as he tumbles to his knees. I move forward, but my legs lock and keep me in place.

"I'll shoot," I threaten the man.

I'm like an annoying fly to this man. He rushes toward Michail and slightly jumps in the air before he brings the sword down on Michail's neck. Blood instantly pours, and the horror tears a scream from my lips. I'm screaming long after Michail hits the ground.

The man is marching toward me, and I pull the trigger several times but nothing happens. I'm staring at the gun, wondering why it won't work. I have no idea and don't get any more time to try again as the man takes a handful of my hair and drags me forward. I don't release the gun until it's kicked from my numb fingers. It slides across the floor and doesn't stop until it hits the skirting board.

He drags me from the bedroom, and as I pass Michail, he gargles for the final time before life leaves his gaze.

We move quickly down the hall as I'm dragged from the bedroom and into the living space.

I'm released without warning and fall to my knees in the middle of the lounge. Air stills in my throat, and all I can think of is what Lucca said earlier about the girls being raped or beaten. Is this how they were being handled?

"Where are my sisters?" I ask, standing up.

Sweat drips off the side of his face. His eyes dart around the space, and he isn't focused anymore.

"Where is he?" he barks, pointing the sword at me.

"I don't know." I want to ask about my sisters again, but he moves closer and brings the sword to my throat. My hands rise into the air like I can stop him from killing me.

"Don't lie to me."

The sword nicks the sensitive skin of my neck. Warm liquid dribbles down, leaving a path of blood that soaks into my top.

"I'm not lying. Please."

The sword is removed from my neck, and he points at the couch. "Sit down and don't try anything."

My legs feel like they are encased in blocks of cement, but when he points the sword at me again, I manage to make my way to the couch.

"Are my sisters dead?" I ask after a few moments of him sweating and pacing in front of me. He glares at me and tightens his hold on the sword.

"Be quiet." His snarl has me sinking further back into the couch. My neck still aches, but I think it's stopped bleeding. I feel petty even thinking about my sore neck when Michail is dead in my bedroom, and what will happen when Lucca walks through that door? Will I have to watch him die before I'm taken?

That thought wraps itself heavily around my shoulders as I sit, waiting for Lucca to come back. The moment the red light appears over the elevator, both the man with the sword and I lean forward. The doors open, and Lucca steps out. He looks up at the man, but his gaze doesn't touch me.

My body starts to tremble, and I want to go to him, but I don't dare move a muscle.

Lucca takes off his jacket slowly, like a man with a sword isn't standing in his lounge.

"I want out." The man with the sword holds it with both hands as he takes two steps in Lucca's direction, but he's smart enough to keep his distance.

Lucca's calm is unsettling, and I don't know if it's that he doesn't care if I die or if this man is no real threat to him.

Lucca hangs his jacket up on a rack, and his gaze touches me. It's quick, but his eyes flicker down to my neck.

"You hurt her," he states.

The man quickly looks at me before frowning back at Lucca. "I want out. That's all I want." He's sweating again. I can see it making a pathway down the side of his face.

"Michail," Lucca calls, and I close my eyes against the image of Michail's gaping throat. I didn't know him, but he was a man, a man who might have a family and didn't deserve to die.

"He's dead." The man shuffles back and forth. "I just wanted to clear the air, but he wouldn't let me. I had no choice. I want out of this."

"You think I have the power to allow you to walk away from this?" Lucca's voice is calm, and he unbuttons the sleeve of his shirt and rolls it up to his forearm.

"You're the fucking Handler."

My heart won't slow, and now as this man swings the sword in a large arc with anger, I'm afraid he'll turn and remember I'm sitting here and slice me to pieces.

The room closes in, and black dots swim around my vision. I dig my nails into my arm, and the sound that had ceased comes flooding back.

"You knew the moment you started this job that there are only two ways out." Lucca takes a side step that brings him closer to me.

"You're not doing yourself any favors, Handler. I can kill you both right now."

"I think you're intelligent enough to know that I can't really grant you what you want." Lucca unbuttons his other sleeve and rolls it up.

"I was only a lookout," the man starts, and there's a dip in his voice.

Lucca nods. "Did you work with Sacha?"

"Yeah."

"He's dead."

I'm staring at Lucca, feeling like he's trying to provoke this guy, who doesn't need any encouragement at all.

The man is shaking his head. "I was just talking to him."

"I was just in his home, and his throat was sliced." Lucca nods at the sword.

"I promise I'll let you leave here with your life if you tell me where the girls are."

The man half laughs. "I don't know. They didn't tell me where they were taking them."

"Who are 'they'?" Lucca asks.

The man is shifting from one leg to the other, making me nervous. I glance behind me. I could slide off the couch and crawl behind it, but if I move, he will notice. He's passing the sword back and forth in his hands.

He's going to kill Lucca and then me. Maybe I'll be first. Would that be easier? Blood starts to roar in my ears, and I'm back in the water. I don't want to go back here, but it's like my mind reboots and sends me there when I can't take much more.

My dad's large arm wraps around my waist, and I'm airborne. I'm laughing. I'm happy. I'm safe.

The light reflects off his silver bracelet, and I blink.

"Nah, I'm not telling you. If I do, they'll kill me."

I'm back in the room, and I don't want to be. Lucca glances at me, and so does the man.

It takes my foggy brain a moment to realize the man is moving toward me. I'm trying to scramble off the couch, waiting for the sword to come down on my back as I try to climb over the back.

My scalp burns as I'm dragged backward. Everything happens so fast. I hear Lucca curse. I'm falling down and crash heavily onto the ground. Pain radiates across my back and steals the air from my lungs. Lucca's shoes shuffle close to me; he's behind the man.

I can't breathe as I watch the struggle. A large dark form falls beside me. His eyes are lifeless, wide open, and bloodshot, and my brain reboots again, only this time I'm not in the water with my dad in County Clare. Instead, I'm falling back into a pit of darkness.

I'm on a ship again; the sway under me is something I'm familiar with. It's a comforting sensation for a brief moment until I sit up fully.

"You're okay."

I follow the hand that touches my shoulder all the way up to Lucca, who's driving.

"You're okay," he reinstates.

My hand automatically goes to my neck. I prod the bandage. "How long have I been out?"

I stare out the window at the deserted landscape around us. "Where are we going?"

A thudding sound from the trunk of the car has me looking behind me. "What the hell is that?"

"Take a breath, Evie."

I sit back, but I don't stay like that for long, as whoever is in the trunk keeps banging.

"I'm hoping he has answers. I found him at Sacha's house."

Lucca removes his hand from me, and I feel the loss instantly.

"You've been asleep about an hour, and we're leaving the city. It's not safe anymore."

I'm nodding. "So, where are we going?" I'm looking out the window, not liking how deserted everything seems.

"To my home," Lucca responds, and when I glance at him, he faces forward. I turn up the radio so I don't have to hear the constant banging from the trunk and hope we find answers to where my sisters are.

CHAPTER NINE

LUCCA

Normally, I only ever go home when I don't have any jobs. It's my time to unwind and spend time with Anita.

I glance at Evie, who's sitting up straight while staring out the window. Even in her frazzled state, she's still beautiful. The gates slowly open, and I drive up to the large house.

"This is your home?"

The front door opens, and Anita smiles when she sees me. Her gaze travels to Evie, and her smile falters only slightly. Instead, I see a lot of questions on my sister's lips.

Once I stop the car, she's marching down the three steps toward the car. Her skin-tight leopard-print suit is my sister's signature clothing.

Evie hasn't moved, and I don't look at her. Most women are very intimidated by my sister. She's a bit of a force, but she constantly looks out for me.

I don't get the door open because she beats me to it.

"You're home?" She raises both eyebrows like I might explain to her why I'm home with a girl. I climb out, and she moves back. The passenger door closes, and Evie steps around the car.

"Hi there, kitten." Anita walks around to Evie, who holds her hand out.

They shake, but the amusement in Anita's face has her brows still raised.

Her bracelets jangle as she takes Evie's hand.

"Hi. I'm Evie."

"Evie, this is my sister, Anita." I introduce them as I close my car door.

Anita links her arm with Evie's. "She's beautiful," she mouths to me silently as she leads Evie into the house.

I want to tell her not to get attached, that this is work.

"You have Lucca's eyes," Evie says to Anita.

The way she says my name is like we're familiar with each other.

"Our mother was a looker. I'm sure yours is, too. Or is it your father?"

I close the front door. "Anita," I warn. She had to turn everything sexual.

She waves me off without looking at me. "You hungry, kitten?"

Evie is the one who looks back at me. "You go with Anita. I'll join you shortly."

Evie nods and leaves. I crane my neck from side to side before removing my jacket and going back to the car.

Dima is awake and back to rattling the trunk. I drive the car around to the back, close to the basement doors.

Once I'm near enough, I unlock the basement doors and get Dima out of the trunk.

He's ready to jump, and I land a solid punch into his face. He cries out, and I use the moment to drag him from the trunk and push him toward the door. He stumbles down the steps and misses the last three. The door closes behind us, but the sensor lights turn on in the basement one section at a time.

A large pole in the center is where I drag a disoriented Dima to. I shove him against it, keeping my hand on his chest. I clip the chains around his waist and chest and don't release him until they are locked.

"Dima, this is your chance to save yourself," I tell him as I roll up my sleeves and push over my trolley, which holds my bag of tools. I roll the kit out slowly and let him see all the objects. "Like everything in life, we can do this the easy way or the hard way. It's up to you."

He spits but doesn't say anything. I take it he isn't talking.

That's how these things normally start out. They end a different way.

I take out a small knife. "That's okay. I don't like to rush in either." I grin as I throw the knife. It grazes his ear and embeds itself in the pole he's tied to.

I pick up another knife and throw it into the air before catching it. I've used these knives since I was a kid. They are like an extension of me.

"I grew up in Camp Cempt."

Fear grows steadily in Dima's eyes. It isn't a known fact about me. I only tell that fact about myself to the people I know will never reveal this about me.

Dima will never get to tell anyone. He will never leave this basement, no matter what he says.

"We were taken into the woods. It was always freezing, not that our beds were warm." I point the knife at Dima. "But they gave us something that the wooded landscape couldn't."

I let the knife fly, and it clips off some of Dima's hair, which sails past his face and lands at his feet. Sweat drips down the side of his face.

"Ask your questions." His voice still holds too much control.

I return to the trolley and pick up another knife. "They gave us an escape from General Obshcheye."

Once again, Dima's fear grows.

"We had to move through the woods without making a sound and hit the targets on the trees with our knives that he had set the night before." I had lived for those moments in the forest.

Dima is glancing around the room.

"I feel insulted, Dima. Here I am sharing something personal, and you look bored."

Dima's gaze returns to me as I release the third knife, which grazes his other ear. Blood trickles down his face.

"I never missed a target. General Obshcheye was a great teacher."

I return and pick up another knife. "Some of the boys were so cold that they weren't able to hold the knives. The noise of the knives hitting the ground spelled their doom."

He broke a boy's arm for dropping his knives. He killed a few during my time at camp.

I release the knife. Dima tries to shift against his chains before a scream of pain pours from his mouth.

The knife sticks out of his calf.

"How long do you think it will take for you to lose enough blood to die?"

Now more fear fills Dima's eyes, and that small amount of anger and control is nearly gone.

"All we had to do was make sure all the security were in one area at a certain time, and all the girls were taken safely off the ship. That was it."

I pretend I don't hear him as I return to my throwing knives.

"What was that boy's name?" I toss the knife a few times into the air. "Maksim." That was it.

I face Dima, whose skin is paling further. "The general had broken his arm only a few months before. This day, it was colder than all the rest."

I grin at Dima. "I'm not going to lie, even I felt the cold."

I toss the knife into the air. "So when Maksim dropped his knives, instead of staying and taking his punishment, he ran." I release the knife, and it embeds itself in his thigh.

His screams feed the beast inside me.

"I swear that's all I did. I have no idea where they took those girls." Drool pours from his mouth; his chin rests on his chest.

I pick up another knife, and he sobs. "The general chased after Maksim, and I remember feeling like I was watching a lion chase a deer. I got a front-row seat, and I couldn't look away." I take a step toward Dima. "I couldn't look away, even as the general grabbed Maksim by the scruff of his neck. The force rattled him like a rag doll."

I reach Dima now and shake him as violently as I can. When I stop, I hold the knife to his eye.

"The general took out his hunting knife."

Dima's eyes grow wide, his face turns gray as he stares at the knife only a millimeter away from his eye.

"I want a name now, Dima."

His breathing is harsh as he stares at the knife. "The Torpedo. That's who we handed the girls over to."

When I don't react, he glances at me. "I swear on my mother's life." He's telling the truth.

"I believe you." I grin, and he starts to half cry but doesn't move. The knife is too close to his eye.

"When the general held that knife to Maksim's eye, I knew he wouldn't drive it all the way through. He would just make him suffer."

Dima's breathing grows more erratic, and I do what the general did. I pierce Dima's eye. His roars are louder than Maksim's were.

The general turned to us all and made us come over one by one to look at the wound. Some boys threw up. I remember when I had stood up to Maksim, so I couldn't help but want to see the wound fully. I forced him to open his eye, inflicting more pain on him.

I ate up the pride in the general's gaze that day.

Dima continues to scream, reminding me my knife is still embedded in his eye. I push the knife all the way in until his screams cease and the air leaves his lungs. Pulling it back out, his head rests on his chest as its final resting place.

I wash and clean my knives as I think about the information Dima has just given me. I don't want it to register, because the outcome isn't looking good. If The Torpedo was behind this kidnapping, and he was in Igor's office the same day as I was, it isn't a stretch to think that Igor had something to do with this also.

The water cleans the blood away from my knives, and I dry them and place them back into their holding places.

Maybe that's why he called me in and not someone else. He knew this wasn't something I had ever dealt with before. But he hadn't counted on all that Evie had seen, all that she was able to tell me.

Without her, I would have been suspicious of Sacha, especially after the autopsy, but I think I would have hit a lot of brick walls.

Once I've cleaned up everything, I release Dima's body from the pole and turn up the furnace, which has been smoldering, and that's where I throw his body. That's how I make every single person disappear. No traces left at all.

★★★

Anita is questioning Evie about her neck when I step into the kitchen. Evie doesn't answer because she becomes aware of my presence.

"I'm going to take Evie to her room. She's had a long day."

Anita wears a permanent grin like she knows I'm full of shit. "You don't look so good yourself."

"Thanks." I don't care as long as I have no blood on my clothes.

"We'll talk more later, kitten." Anita winks at Evie, who gets up and smiles down at her.

"Thank you." Evie's appreciation is expressed with the hand she touches my sister's with.

I let them have their moment before I lead Evie upstairs.

I'm ready to take her to a guest room, but instead, I pass all the closed doors and lead her to my own room.

The minute I enter, I start to strip off my tie.

"I got a name. I know who has the girls. I don't know where they are yet, but I have a name." I'm not facing Evie when I tell her this. I pause in unbuttoning my shirt and turn before I resume doing it.

"How?" She's smiling at me. Her smile is the reason smiles are created, to show someone that you are happy. It makes me feel unsettled with her.

"I got the information out of the man in the trunk." I peel off my shirt, and her smile falters slightly as she takes her time and admires me.

"What if he tells the people on you?"

"He won't." I kick off my shoes.

Evie tilts her head like she's trying to add that up, but something else fills her eyes. I can't tell what it is as she steps up to me.

"Thank you, Lucca."

"I'm being paid to do this, remember?"

I step away from Evie, not liking at all how she's looking at me. Her small, warm fingers grip my wrist.

In spite of knowing better, the longing in her eyes has me turning to face her. She makes me curious.

"Still, thank you for finding my sisters."

I don't think she will be thanking me when I'm handing them over along with her.

She lowers her lids but keeps an innocent smile on her lips. For a split second, I think she's trying to manipulate me into something, but the thought flees as she rises up on the tips of her toes and gives me the sweetest kiss that has ever touched my lips.

She presses a second kiss to my lips, and this time I grip her shoulders. "What are you doing?"

Her cheeks heat up, but her gaze doesn't waver from mine. She shrugs. "I'm just…" She licks her lips, her small pink tongue too enticing to ignore.

I drag her into me and kiss her like I really want to. My hand grips her waist. She doesn't move under my lips for a millisecond, and then she responds.

I'm moving her back to the bed, my cock growing harder at the thought of being inside a virgin.

A kiss won't satisfy me. It won't quench the thirst Evie leaves in my throat.

I break the kiss and reach down, tugging her top up over her head. Her large breasts fill the black bra, just like I pictured.

Her eyes are wild, and I see the hesitation, so I kiss her again while gripping her large breasts and squeezing them slightly. She gasps at the contact, and when I lay her on the bed, she tries to push me away.

I don't get off her, but I do break the kiss reluctantly.

"I can't…" she starts, and I grin at her.

"I know I can't fuck you, Evie, but we can do other things."

I want to fuck her, but I don't think she's ready for that, or I'm not ready to face the consequences of doing that to her.

"What other things?" she asks while I press a kiss to her lips before getting off her.

I pull her skirt off, and she looks even more glorious than I remember. The memory is pretty good, but the real thing has me pulling off my trousers.

Fear enters her eyes, and instead of comforting her, I pull down my boxers too and let her see my erection. Her running now isn't a bad idea. I just said I wouldn't fuck her, but I'm not sure if I can really hold back. She shifts on the bed, and I think she's going to leave, but instead, she reaches back and removes her bra, allowing her large breasts to fall free. Her nipples are hard, and before she changes her mind, I dip my head and capture one in my mouth. Her groan is instant, and I reach to pull her panties off. Her small hand covers mine.

I continue to suck her nipple and run my teeth along the delicate skin until her hand slips from mine, and I grip the small piece of fabric and tug it down.

I release her nipple to remove her panties and take a look at her neat pussy that nestles in perfectly between her thighs.

More fear and uncertainty fill her gaze, and I don't wait for her to reconsider again, so I capture her other nipple in my mouth while reaching down and touching her bud, which feels swollen with want under my fingertips.

CHAPTER TEN

EVIE

What am I doing? The thought keeps coming and going. When he isn't touching me, I know I need to get dressed and away from this man. But each time he touches me, I lose myself in his arms.

I kissed him when he told me he had a lead. Now that we're closer to getting them back, I need Lucca on my side so he will let them go free.

It's a big ask, and at first, I thought of giving him my virginity. But now, being here under him, I know I need to stop this.

His tongue swirls around my nipple, and the dampness is heavy between my legs. His manhood looks so much bigger than I expected it to be. That would hurt. I'm sure of it.

Lucca's lips find me, and his kiss is quick and sharp. His kisses are bruising, and I should stop this, but I'm kissing him back, following what he does.

His erection is pressed against my thigh. I keep considering touching it to please him, but fear keeps my hands on his shoulders. I want to be brave enough to tease him, but I'm not.

Not that he needs me to entice him. His fingers fall lower, closer to my opening, and my legs open slightly on their own accord. Lucca stops and looks at me.

The silver of his eyes is a dark, stormy gray. All his muscles seem more prominent, and he climbs off the bed.

"Don't move." The warning is quick, but as he leaves me lying naked on the bed, I'm tempted to reach down and get my clothes. I sit up.

"Don't move," he repeats, reappearing with a jar in his hand.

"What is that?" I ask.

He doesn't answer but climbs back on the bed, leaving the jar on the bed beside us. I'm trying to read the label when he kisses me again and pushes me back down. This time, his manhood is positioned right at my opening. It's terrifying, but right now, I've never felt more alive.

Reaching down, Lucca takes his erection in his hand and rubs it against me. It causes a ripple that grows and amplifies through my body, and when he nips my nipple, I cry out at all the different sensations.

"I want to fuck you," Lucca whispers in my ear before biting my earlobe, and he spins me around. His body is hard against me, and he reaches around to my front and grips my breasts.

I'm aware of every single place our flesh touches. The dampness between my legs is growing as he pushes himself against my back opening.

I glance to my left as he picks up the jar.

A warm, oily substance is rubbed into my back passage, and I'm trying to pull away.

"It's okay. It will be nice," Lucca says, and his fingers move in circles around my opening. I don't want to like it, but it's sending electricity throughout my whole body. It feels like too much. All of it feels like too much, but I don't want him to stop.

He presses a finger against my back opening, and it sinks in. I look at him over my shoulder. He's gripping his large penis in his hand, moving it back and forth as he pushes his finger deeper into my ass.

When he removes his finger, I can't look away as he covers his manhood in the oily substance and strokes it a few more times. I'm on all fours and facing forward as he moves in behind me. My body tenses with fear, waiting for pain, but he only rests his erection at my back passage as he reaches around and touches me.

The dampness that had been drying up comes back again, and when his other hand grips my breasts, my body relaxes. I feel him push into me.

"Lucca." I want this, but I don't know what's happening.

"Enjoy it." He pushes deeper, and when he grows, my body tightens and relaxes over and over again.

I stop fighting this and close my eyes as he goes deeper into my back passage. He's moving slowly, but his hand is working at my front, and I'm panting as my body tightens and relaxes, the sensations growing more and more intense. I want more, but I don't know if I can take it.

Without uttering a word, Lucca pushes himself deeper inside me, and I can't stop the instant pleasure that takes over me, and I call out his name again as I come.

He removes himself from my ass, and I'm trying to catch myself as I turn to see him touching his manhood. A creamy white substance pours from the head and all over my ass. It's warm and thick, and I'm awed by the look on his face. Power roars through my veins as we stare at each other. I never thought it would feel this way to have someone touch me and make me come. I most certainly never thought watching someone else come could be so rewarding.

Lucca stops stroking himself and grins at me. My heart starts to rise again as his grin turns into a smile I've never seen before, and I'm smiling back at him.

He climbs off the bed, then leans in and scoops me up. Wrapping my arms around his neck, I study his face as he carries me into the bathroom. It's not as grand as the penthouse, but it's his. Bottles of shower gel and hair products are on a stand in the shower he puts my feet down into. He turns on the water, and I take a moment to check him out. Even his bum is solid. Warm water flicks close to me.

"Take your time," Lucca says before stepping out of the shower. I step into the spray of water and start to wash.

I feel like a woman. I remember the first time I bled. It was terrifying and painful, but afterward, I felt like a real woman. That's exactly how this feels now, like I'm a fully-fledged woman.

I take my time and wash my body. I touch my ass, expecting it to be sore, but it's just sensitive to the touch. They didn't teach us that on the ship.

I finish washing, and when I return to the bedroom, Lucca isn't there. I feel disappointed until I see fresh clothes have been laid out on the bed for me.

A pair of dark jeans and a purple top lie on the bed. My bra is on the floor, and I pick it up and start to get dressed. I'm tempted to look around the room to learn more about Lucca, but he enters the room with wet hair from a recent shower. He is redressed in black trousers and a white shirt. His silver eyes look stark.

I know my intentions for kissing him were so I could convince him to free my sisters, but at his first touch, something shifted, and now I want to know more about Lucca. I want to know the man I wanted.

"I'm from Ireland."

Lucca runs his hand through his dark hair but pauses at my words.

"I had this weird obsession with swimming at night. My parents warned me about the current, but…" I shrug and sit down on the bed. "I didn't listen to them."

Lucca steps into the room.

"This one night, I found a girl. She was about my age."

I want Lucca to ask me questions. I want him to become invested in me. If I can make him see me as a person and not a thing, I might have a chance at saving my sisters.

"Her boat had washed up on our shoreline. I tried to help her, but I got dragged into the water and was knocked unconscious." I swallow the pain that feels like it was only inflicted yesterday.

"I was ten. I was stolen from the shores of County Clare, from my parents." Pain burns my chest and tightens around my heart. Lucca is watching me, but he isn't reacting.

"The girl I tried to save was recaptured by the men who had stolen her from her home. They made an example of her, a warning to the rest of us not to run. She died at my feet." I blink from the tears and let them fall. The pain is still so raw. "I died there, too," I whisper.

"I'm sorry." Lucca isn't sorry. His words are empty.

"I was a child." I'm standing now, trying to connect with the humanity that is in us all.

He doesn't speak, and I can see I'm losing any sympathy I had.

"You asked me who I was trying to ring. You still want to know?"

He doesn't. I can see it in his eyes.

"My parents, in Ireland. Who, to this day, I'm sure are still looking for their ten-year-old daughter."

My lip trembles, and I bite down on it. "They could drain the sea, and they won't find me, Lucca." I move closer to him. "Can you understand that kind of pain?"

He doesn't answer.

"Times that by seven. Six more of my sisters were taken. Sold. And you have the power to set us all free."

I wipe falling tears off my face.

"I'm sorry that you suffered, Evie. But my job is to return you all to Igor."

His voice is emotionless.

"You don't care that they steal children?"

"It happens. It's life. You should really count yourself lucky that you didn't end up somewhere far worse."

His words are like a slap in the face.

"You must have had a very cushy life. It's fine for people like you that lost nothing."

Lucca takes a step toward me. "I have lost plenty, Evie. But my loss won't make me see yours any differently than what it is."

"What is your loss?" I'm clenching my fists with frustration. I'm trying to find a connection with him. He's reacting to everything with only indifference and calm. "You're full of lies," I spit.

His head tilts, and the warning is there to be very careful.

I swallow my anger and close my eyes while nodding my head.

"I grew up in a camp from the age of six."

I open my eyes, and my heart sinks. Six. Too young. "I'm so sorry." I don't hold back my horror at the thoughts of a young Lucca in some camp.

"Most of the boys there were also stolen."

I sink back onto the bed. "You were stolen, too."

His indifference makes sense now. He doesn't want to feel.

He moves for the first time. "No. I volunteered. I'm not like you, Evie. I wasn't stolen or taken. I was there because that's where I wanted to be. I enjoyed the training and being the best. I watched plenty of boys die for their weakness. It is what it is."

I can't believe that. I can't believe that someone could be that cold about a life.

"And Anita? Was she raised at this camp?"

Lucca runs his hands through his hair again. "No. It was only for boys. She was with my parents."

"They didn't mind you going to a training camp?"

"No." His answer is abrupt. "Did you really think that by allowing me to fuck your ass I would do as you wish?"

The grin that graces his stunning face is cold and chills me to the bone.

"You don't have to be so crude."

His laughter is like hailstones against my flesh. I just want him to stop.

"You think that's crude? They really sheltered you. You're naïve to the point that it's dangerous."

I stand up. "I kissed you so you might help me," I admit.

His grin turns into a snarl.

"But then you touched me, and my intentions became something very different. I wanted you to touch me. So, I didn't allow you to have me"—I refused to repeat his words—"just to get you to do my bidding. I just hoped by telling you what happened to me that you would see me as a human and not a thing."

My honesty has the grin slipping from his face. "I do see you, Evie. But it changes nothing."

For the first time, I detect a lie. It's small, but it's there. He does see me as something more than a job, and that will change everything.

CHAPTER ELEVEN

LUCCA

I don't run. I want to, and I don't understand fully what that means for me. So I keep my feet planted. I've come up against some of the most dangerous men in the Bratva. I've been in deadly situations since I was a kid. So, I'm not going to let this tiny woman have me running with my tail between my legs.

I want her to see the logic in what she's asking, but I don't want to address it, either.

Her wet hair hangs down her back, and her blue eyes are so bright that I want to promise her the stars, the moon, and the sun. The bastards stole her as a child.

I run both my hands through my hair like I can push that image out of my mind, what she must have witnessed. Yet, she looked so innocent, like she'd never seen a violent act.

"Does your sister have kids?" she asks, and a part of me admires her perseverance, while another wants her to shut up.

"No." I keep it to one-word answers as best I can.

"If it were my daughter…" Her gaze waters over again. "I'd never stop looking for her, Lucca." My name is a tug to my heart that I refuse to allow her to see.

"If it were my daughter, I'd never stop. My dad will never stop. Eight years."

"I think Igor needs to know how traitorous you really are." My words have the desired effect on her, and she pales, yet I don't feel the level of satisfaction I should. "You really think that I care."

Tears fall from her stunning eyes, but I continue. "You really think I'd give up everything I have because I'm attracted to you."

"No, Lucca. I thought you might help because you're human."

She wipes her tears away.

"Everyone is human, Evie. The ones that took you, the ones that sold girls, the ones who even raped and abused them."

She flinches.

"I can't help you."

She covers her mouth like she can keep in her pain, but I watch it spill down her face, and I have the urge to run from the room, but I don't.

"I will find your sisters." I just hope they're alive.

"And hand them back to Igor." The sound of her snarl makes it easier to grin. This time I leave the room knowing I'm leaving a mark on her, and that she should stop asking me to care.

Anita is outside the bedroom door with one hand on her hip. Before she even considers going off on one of her rants, I grip her arm and steer her toward the stairs.

"Does this have anything to do with Nicolai?"

Nicolai is The Collector. He collects people and drops them off to the bosses. Most don't want to be collected; most are never seen again. I helped Nicolai out a few months back. He had fallen for one of the boss's daughters, and I wasn't sure he survived the exchange. To hear he was alive was a relief. We had spent time in prison together, and when you survive a Russian prison, you never forget.

"Why would you ask about Nicolai?" I ask Anita once we clear the final step.

She pulls away from my touch and spins to face me. She's pissed.

"Nicolai rang looking for you. Are you involved in human trafficking? I can handle a lot of shit, Lucca. But not that."

My sister's head is moving from side to side. I know better than to dismiss her.

"That's not what I do. Nor does Nicolai."

My sister calms. "But that girl up there was…?" She raises both eyebrows as she waits for an answer.

"You're my sister, Anita. And I love you. But keep away from Evie."

I'm ready to end this conversation, but Anita isn't.

"Like *you* kept away? It didn't sound like that when I passed your room earlier."

"What I do in my home is my business," I remind Anita.

Anita's ready to argue back.

"You know this world. She'll be gone soon."

Anita huffs and walks away.

After closing my office door, I ring Nicolai.

"You survived Mila's father?" I ask.

"I barely survived Mila. She had to shoot me."

I laugh at the image of Nicolai being shot by a small female. "Had to? Or was she just sick of you?"

"Her father made her shoot me, or he would. A story for another day."

Nicolai's tone grows serious, and I'm ready to hear what he rang me about. We don't contact each other unless we need help. I'm knee-deep in all this with Evie, but I'll still help Nicolai.

"I heard you got an investigation job," Nicolai starts.

"You have information that can help, brother?" I ask back.

We aren't blood related, but after all we've been through together, he's more a brother to me than if the same blood pumped through our veins.

"The Torpedo was spotted at a ball for auctioning off virgins," he says. "Most of the buyers were from Saudi Arabia, and we know how they like to spend their money. I heard of a lot of movement from oil giants coming here but brushed it off until I heard you were on the hunt for a group of girls."

I've been so focused on other aspects of this that I hadn't asked about anything else. I'm pissed I didn't hear about the oil giants' movements, especially ones from Saudi Arabia. Along with the ball, these are things I should have been looking for."

"This isn't your territory. But I have men keeping their ears to the ground who will inform me of any more movement. You're in luck, that's why I was ringing. I thought reports of women being held in a warehouse would interest you."

"Thanks, brother. I owe you."

"I'll send you the address," Nicolai finishes.

Now that I'm close to finishing this job, I'm also closer to handing Evie back.

Silence drags out along the other line of the phone.

"You need me to do something, you know all you have to do is ask," I say.

"Actually, I do."

I wait to hear what he needs me for.

"I'm getting married and need a best man."

I sit back in the chair and grin. "Who is she?" I ask.

"Mila."

"I'll be there."

More silence, and I know Nicolai isn't finished.

"So will a lot of the Bratva. Like The Torpedo."

"Don't have him as a groomsman. He might not be able to make it." If it came to a head-on situation with The Torpedo and he didn't give in, it would be a fight to the death, and I have no intention of losing.

"Just think about my wedding before you kill him."

I half laugh before I grow serious again. "I'll keep that in mind. Give my congrats to Mila."

"I will. If I hear anything else, I'll let you know."

"Thanks, brother." I end the call, and my phone beeps in my pocket.

I take it out and read the address of where the warehouse is. It's only twenty to thirty minutes away. I gather all I need, my throwing knives and two guns, and make sure they're ready and loaded before I go upstairs.

Evie is still in my bedroom. She quickly closes my wardrobe door like she wasn't snooping. I don't say anything, and when she faces me, she raises a brow. It's an expression that's very sexy on her.

The thought of having her again has me softening my tone before I start to speak.

"I got a call from a friend. I might know where the girls are."

Her mouth opens slightly, and she takes a step toward me. "Really? Are they alive? Did he say what condition they're in?"

I hold up my hand to stop the next question that's ready to fly from her lips.

"I don't know, Evie. All I have is an address."

"I'm coming." She's looking around the floor until she spots her shoes.

"No, you're not."

She slips them on, much to my irritation.

"I can calm the girls down when we find them. I'm sure they're terrified."

"I can manage, Evie."

She finishes putting on her shoes. "Please, Lucca. Let me be there for my sisters. If I can't do anything else, at least let me do this."

"I said no." My words are final. I won't allow her to come. I have no idea what I'm walking into, and I'm most certainly not putting her in danger.

"Leah—she's fragile."

I nod at Evie, hating the look of defeat on her face, but I need to leave now.

Anita is in the hallway when I come downstairs.

"Why is there so much security everywhere? Is it because of Evie?"

"No. It's just a precaution," I tell Anita as I take my suit jacket off the rack.

As I slip it on, Anita slams a hand on her hip. "A precaution from what?"

"From people."

She rolls her eyes. "Always so vague."

I press a kiss to my sister's cheek, and she relaxes immediately. "You have nothing to worry about. You're safe."

Thirty security men may have been overkill, but with my sister and Evie in the same house, I'm not risking them for a second.

"I won't be long."

Anita doesn't ask me any more questions, and I leave and make my way to the warehouse.

It takes me twenty-five minutes, and when I pull up at the abandoned location, I sit for a moment and take in the surroundings—checking street corners for cameras and the foot traffic to gauge how many people might have seen something. So far, I don't see any cameras, and there is only one shop that appears open, but it's hard to tell with the painted front window. No one passes along the block, and I get out of the car.

The alleyway is filled with rubbish and junk, but there is a clear path for a vehicle to drive down. Once I reach the end of the alleyway, a chain-link fence runs across most of the front area of the warehouse; a small gap at the end is how I enter. The red brick building is old, and I look up at the three floors but don't see any movement. Crows land on the rooftop, caw, and fly off. That's the only sign of life so far.

Steps lead up to a large solid door, and I climb them, but the door doesn't budge.

I return to the yard. A large roller door at the far end of the building is slightly open. A plastic barrel is keeping it up; regardless of whether it was left there intentionally or lodged by mistake, I dip down and look in. The space isn't dark; plenty of light from yellow-tinted windows pours into the enormous space. I roll under the door and stand up with a gun in hand. I listen before I start to move. Barrels are stacked everywhere, and I move carefully around them. Another large chain-link fence has been set up in the center of the warehouse. The large square is coated in black sacks, but some of them have ripped away, which allows me to see several dirty mattresses on the ground.

The girls must have been here, but they aren't anymore.

A chain that keeps the fence together lies on the ground. I move through the small gap. The black sacks on either side rustle as I step into the space. I count six mattresses, and at each, a set of chains. Old food sits at the end of the beds.

Blood on one set of chains has me thinking of Evie, imagining her chained here and forced to lie on a dirty mattress. I leave the small pit and look around the rest of the ground floor of the warehouse.

I slip my gun back into the band of my trousers and get ready to leave when five men step out from behind the rows of barrels, blocking me from leaving.

They circle me, and I glance at each of them and take in their positions just like I was trained to do. I only needed to keep one alive. The rest can die.

I raise my hands slowly and bring them to the back of my neck, where two of my throwing blades are positioned. The five men hold their swords at the ready as I dip down like I'm ready to surrender and fall to my knees.

I take the knives in my hands and let them fly from both sides of me. They hit their targets perfectly. The general would have been proud. The other three charge, and I remove two more from their pouches in the band of my trousers. I'm running sideways away from them, and when I reach the barrels, I turn and launch one at the first man. It embeds itself in the man's forehead, taking him down. The two other men have to dance across him, and it gives me a moment to pull out my gun.

I dodge a sword that cracks into the barrel and dance away while releasing my knife, which embeds itself into the man's arm. It slows him down but doesn't stop him and the last man from charging.

Something catches my leg, and I hit the ground hard and roll as the blade sparks across the ground. Once I stop rolling, I fire two shots into the man's face.

The last man disappears behind the barrels. He's one I need alive. I stand up to see it's a bundle of ropes I tripped across.

"If you give me some answers, I'll let you live," I say, holding my gun and watching for him to rise from the barrels.

Silence screams back at me, and I turn in time to see him. He charges me with his raised sword. I bend, but it slices into my cheek, and I empty the gun into his face while moving away.

My face is on fire, and I curse him as I remove my jacket and press it to my cheek to slow down the bleeding.

Every man is dead. I have no one to question. I move around the bodies and gather up my throwing knives while checking them for ID, tattoos, or anything that could identify them, but I find nothing on any of the bodies.

Once outside, I take the jacket away from my face, and the wind sends more pain slicing across my cheek. Blood still oozes from the wound, but I don't think it's at a dangerous level.

Taking my phone out of my pocket, I consider ringing Nicolai. He would come, but he isn't the man for the job. I had grown up with Nev at camp, and he became a very famous tracker. He doesn't work for anyone in particular, but if the price is right, he will do the job.

I dial his number.

Heavy breathing on the phone makes me think I've rang the wrong number until I hear his deep voice.

"I'm in the middle of something." He sounds like he's jogging. "What do you want?"

The fact he answered makes me continue.

"I have an urgent job I need you for."

"Message me the details and price, and I'll let you know." He hangs up, and I pocket my phone.

My face aches as I make my way back down the alleyway. Boxes move, and I withdraw my gun, my finger on the trigger. A dirty face that has old gray eyes staring out at me has me putting the gun away.

"You live here?" I ask the guy, pressing my jacket against my face again.

His weary eyes are focused on the band of my trousers, where my gun disappeared. "Sure do."

I take the jacket away from my face and wince.

"Did you see anything lately?" I point at the warehouse. "Anyone at the warehouse?"

He nods but doesn't answer—his gaze darts to my pockets. I take out my wallet and get two fifties out.

He snatches them from my fingers. His hands are covered in gloves that I am sure would stand on their own with the dirt on them.

"A white van left there only minutes before you arrived. They loaded a group of girls into the back. They sure were beauties."

"You get the license plate number?"

His gaze darts to my pocket again.

I grin. He has to survive. I take my wallet back out and take out two more fifties. He tilts his head, and I add a third.

Reaching out, he snatches the money, his eyes growing brighter as he holds the bills tightly in his hand.

"The plate?" I ask again.

"Didn't get it." He quickly pockets his money.

I'm ready to take my money back when he holds up his hands.

"I did see the man who loaded the women into the van."

He describes a man I haven't seen before. But with a large tattoo on his neck, it might lead me to something.

"You sure?" I ask him before I get ready to leave.

"Yeah, he had a tattoo of a gun and large red cigars on either side of it. It ran along his neck. He was mean looking."

I leave the homeless man, who disappears behind his boxes, and get into the car.

I don't start the engine but look back at the warehouse. How long would it take for them to find out the men they left behind are dead?

I take out my phone and message Nev the job. I describe the man with the tattooed neck and also The Torpedo. I also offer him a generous amount of money I don't think he'll refuse. Once it's sent, I check my face in the mirror.

Fuck

This is going to leave a scar. There's no way it won't. I pull the wound apart to see how deep it is. It needs stitches. Blood oozes again, and I release the skin before starting the car and making my way back to the house.

I drive slowly around the block, just checking for cameras again in case I missed them the first time. But if there were ever cameras here, they're long gone now. I don't imagine much survives in this area.

CHAPTER TWELVE

EVIE

I've felt weak a few times in my life. Even at ten, I understood weakness. When you have to stand and watch someone die, you understand there's nothing you can do about it.

The first time I was marked, I felt weak, knowing I couldn't stop them from branding me.

Letting Lucca walk out that door without me and leaving my sisters in his hands made me feel weak again.

I hold my head high and try to remind myself of all I have survived. All I will survive.

I stay in Lucca's room for a while. I'm tempted to go downstairs and find Anita, but each time I'm ready to step out into the hall, a security man passes, driving me back inside. Looking out the window, I spot a few security men scattered around the front yard. The amount of security should make me feel more secure, but it doesn't. It just feels suffocating right now.

"You okay, kitten?" Anita steps into the bedroom. She's wearing trousers and a black-and-white polka dot shirt. The band in her hair is the same fabric and design as her outfit. She looks glamorous but cheap.

But it's the kindness that pours from her that I cling to.

"No," I answer honestly.

She enters the room. "Anything I can help with?"

I'm ready to tell her no. I don't think she will help me leave, or Lucca wouldn't have left me with her, but she could help me in another way.

"It's Lucca," I start.

She pulls at one of the large loops on her ear before sitting down on the bed. "Isn't it always?" Her smile is similar to his.

"He was telling me about growing up in camp, and it hurt my heart."

Anita grows serious, and I think I've taken this in the wrong direction.

"He told you about camp?" Disbelief coats her words.

"Yes. It sounded brutal."

She nods, and her silver eyes darken. I take the moment to sit down beside her.

"My brother is so strong."

I take her hand in mine. "You must have missed him so much."

"I did. He was like a father to me. Our own was an absolute waste of space." Anita pulls at her earring again and rolls her eyes. Her gaze has lightened like she's referred to her father as that a million times.

"He spent our whole lives behind bars."

I nod like I knew that.

"My mother always believed that was why Lucca went to the camp. That he wanted to be the man our father never was."

It's a drop in the ocean. It's small, minor, some might even say insignificant, information, but the fact it's about Lucca is enough to try to connect the dots.

"Your mother—is she still alive?" I ask.

Anita releases my hand and shakes her head. "She died a few years back."

"I'm sorry for your loss."

"Thanks, kitten." Anita stands, and I think that's all the information I'm going to get out of her.

"What about you? Your parents in the land of the living?"

The question has a hand reaching in and squeezing my heart. I always believed they were, that one day they would find me. I believed that for eight years, that my dad would come and take me back to the shore of County Clare.

"I don't know."

Anita is staring at me like she's waiting for me to expand, but I have no idea what more I can add to that statement.

"You hungry?" she asks.

I'm not, but I find myself nodding my head. I sit in the large spacious kitchen as she makes us a sandwich. I'm stuck in my head for a while, and we eat in silence. We both glance as security moves every few minutes past the door.

Anita rolls her eyes. "Lucca being dramatic."

I smile at her words. I didn't think Lucca could ever be dramatic. He was the least dramatic person I ever met.

It's like my thoughts of Lucca conjure him as he pauses outside the kitchen.

Anita is up.

"What the hell happened to you?"

Lucca waves her off and turns to me. "Take your sandwich to your room." He sounds angry with me, and I'm not sure why. I don't pick up the sandwich but get up.

His face is cut pretty bad, and I want answers about my sisters. This doesn't install much confidence in me.

"My sisters?" I ask.

"Sisters?" Anita repeats, her head jerking between Lucca and me, the large earring swinging widely.

"They weren't there," Lucca answers me, and my legs grow weak.

"You're lying," I fire back. I want it to be a lie.

"I said they weren't there, Evie." He turns away from me, and I'm moving toward him. He spins back around before I reach him. "They had been there, but they aren't now."

A lump forms in my throat, and an ache in my heart has me fighting the burning sensation at the back of my nose.

"You were attacked?" I reach up but don't touch his face.

"It's a flesh wound," he answers.

Anita lets out a heavy breath, and I step away from her brother.

"You look like you went a few rounds with Jackie Chan."

Lucca holds up his hands, a serious expression on his face, and Anita falls silent.

Lucca leaves the room, and I follow him. He glances back at me several times but doesn't stop me as I follow him into the bathroom. The blood staining the front of his shirt still leaks from the cut on his face.

Lucca opens a glass cabinet and takes down some disinfectant wipes, along with some adhesive strips, and places them on the sink.

"Let me help." I don't wait for him to agree but reach around him for the disinfectant wipes. I meet his gaze in the mirror, and he holds it for a moment before turning to me.

He still hasn't moved. "Do you want to sit down?" He's so much taller than I am, and at this angle, it won't be easy.

"No." His jaw tightens.

I take out a wipe and step closer to Lucca until I'm surrounded by the smell of his cologne. His large hands hang at his side, and I try to focus on the task at hand.

I dab the wipe carefully across his cheek. The cut is deep, the skin puckered. I continue to clean the wound in silence before getting the strips and placing them across the cut, keeping it sealed. Lucca doesn't move a muscle as I bandage him up.

"What did you find?" I finally ask, placing the second to last strip on his cheek.

"They were in the warehouse."

My fingers falter, and I look into liquid silver eyes.

"I found where they had been sleeping. They were all together."

Pain radiates across my body. I didn't think the idea of them still together would make me feel homesick, but it does.

I pick up the final strip and press it to Lucca's cheek.

"Do you think…" I look back up into Lucca's eyes. "Do you think they're still alive?"

"They are too valuable to kill."

My stomach churns at the honesty of his words.

"So yes, I do believe they are alive."

"You were attacked? Did you find out anything from your attacker?"

I'm praying that he did, but Lucca turns away from me and faces the mirror. "You did a neat job."

His remark on my bandaging him up shouldn't have any impact on me, but it does.

"Thank you."

Lucca faces me. There's a vulnerable look in his eyes like I've never seen before, and my heart starts to race.

"The men who attacked me are all dead. I didn't get to question them."

My stomach squeezes at the thoughts of him killing someone. But I'm not stupid. I knew that, but it was something I had pushed to the back of my mind, along with so much more.

"There was a man who saw the girls being placed into a van." Lucca breaks eye contact and starts to remove his bloody shirt.

My heart thumps painfully in my chest. The girls are strong. We had already come through the worst. But Leah isn't like us. She's fragile. I can imagine her being placed in a van, maybe blindfolded. She would be terrified, but the other girls would take care of her. They have to.

"I'm sorry, Evie." Lucca's words have my head whipping up to him.

He sounds so sincere, which isn't like him.

Heavy footsteps have Lucca moving me aside. I follow to see Anita in the bedroom.

"Igor is here." Worry is etched into her words. Lucca moves past his sister and removes his shirt before placing a new one on.

"He's here to take me back," I say. I knew this day would come. But now that he's here in Lucca's house, fear squeezes my throat and the room tilts. I reach for the wall. "Please." The air grows thin, and I have no idea what I'm begging him to do.

Lucca won't look at me as he puts on his shirt.

"Lucca." I plead his name, but he still won't look at me. Too many things swirl through my mind. I don't want to leave Lucca is one thought, which is crazy. But being with him gives me hope that I might get out of being sold.

Frustration claws up my throat, and I want to lash out.

"Stay with Evie. Don't come out of this room no matter what."

Lucca's words to his sister pierce my veil of pure panic. I'm not going down. He's leaving me up here. It doesn't mean he won't come back, but it gives me time to convince Anita not to let them take me.

Lucca leaves the room. Anita is staring at the door before she turns to me.

"I'm going to be sold," I tell her.

She doesn't respond, but she looks out of place as she pulls at her loopy earrings.

"I'm a virgin. That's what they're selling me for." I push away from the wall.

Anita shakes her head, wild curls bouncing everywhere. "He won't let them take you."

Her words have no force behind them, and I half laugh and half cry.

"You think he will stop Igor?"

"I don't know, Evie." Anita turns away from me, and I don't want her to ignore me.

"You can help me." I move around her so I'm looking at her. "Please! You can help me get out of here."

She's shaking her head. "You really picked the wrong girl." Anita looks at me with sympathy in her eyes. "I'm sorry, but I would never betray my brother."

"I'm being trafficked, along with six other girls."

She turns away, but I don't stop.

"They took me at the age of ten."

Her shoulders are hunched like she can fend off my words.

"They took me from my parents." My voice breaks.

"They stole me." I want to scream it at the top of my lungs so she will listen.

"They stole all of us. How is that right?"

Anita swings around. "It's not." Her voice rises. "But, I'm sorry. I can't help you."

I blink and tears fall. I'm looking at the window, and for a split second, I think about opening it and jumping. Would I break my legs, my neck? Would it be a better fate than being sold? Or would I land on my feet?

I move to the window. Anita doesn't stop me, but I can see why she doesn't care. The yard has security everywhere and not just Lucca's but also Igor's men.

I turn back to Anita, who is watching me. I think if I had the power to help someone, I would do it. I wouldn't be like Anita.

My mind trails back to the moment in the loading bay when I huddled behind the crates, ready to leave my sisters behind. My cheeks grow red. I didn't take them with me, but I would have sent help. That much I know.

I hold my head and jut out my chin at Anita. "You are as bad as the rest of them." I say my words clearly before sitting on the bed to await my fate.

CHAPTER THIRTEEN

LUCCA

Igor is in the lounge sitting down on a large claw-legged armchair. Three security men surround his seat.

"Igor, what a pleasure to have you in my home." I don't like this man being here for one second. The idea that he's here for Evie has crossed my mind, but he wouldn't come himself instead of sending a lieutenant, so this is something more.

"How is Evie?" he starts with. He's really watching my reaction.

I sit down across from him. His first question should have been what happened to my face, so this was all carefully orchestrated.

"She's upstairs. Shall I bring her down?" I ask.

His down-turned lips turn up slightly. "Just us for now."

I sit fully back in the chair.

"Someone will collect her tomorrow."

My gut tightens. "Perfect."

"A doctor will have to examine her first to make sure she is still pure. No offense."

"None taken," I answer, but the thoughts of Evie being assessed like that have me wanting to walk away from Igor.

His smile shifts, and his lips drag back down. "I know she is a temptation that even the strongest would have to fight."

"I've been too busy, Igor, with my job."

Igor nods and touches his cheek. "I see you got hurt."

"It comes with the territory." I keep my tone respectful, but nothing about this meeting seems appropriate to me.

Igor is watching me, and the fact that he's here tells me he's part of this somehow.

He sits forward suddenly, reaching into his suit jacket and extracting a piece of paper. He leans across the space, not close enough for me to take it. I have to get up and move across the room. He releases the piece of paper, which I then open. It has a name scrawled across it.

"I want him found and silenced."

I sit back down. "No problem. I'll get onto it once I close this case."

Igor rises, and so do I. As he steps closer to me, his security team mirrors his actions. "No need. You're off this case. Consider it closed, and I will have Evie collected tomorrow."

He points at the piece of paper in my hand. "Just focus on this job."

He tries to walk away but pauses. "Oh, and don't worry, you will still get paid for both jobs."

I wasn't going to mention money.

"So, you found the girls?" I ask, knowing it's a mistake when he looks at me with a smirk.

"I'll be in touch tomorrow." Igor leaves, and I watch him from the sitting room window as his men climb into three separate cars and drive away from my house.

Evie will be collected tomorrow. None of this sits right with me. If Igor is already over this operation, what could he gain from planning a kidnapping? None of it makes sense.

I go upstairs, and the moment I open the bedroom door, Evie spins away from the window and stares at me. She's pale, but I see a flicker of hope in her blue eyes.

Anita raises both brows, waiting on an answer as to why Igor came to our home.

"He was just checking in." The lie is quick to leave my lips, and I don't focus on my sister but Evie.

"He drove this whole way just to check in?"

"There are millions on the table, Evie, so yes, he did."

"I'll leave you to it."

I glance at Anita over my shoulder. "Thanks."

She nods at me, takes one final worrying look at Evie, and leaves. Now I wonder what transpired between the two women.

"Is Igor your only boss?" I ask the most important question. I'm thinking he isn't in this alone, and maybe he is stealing from another partner.

Evie shakes her head. "No."

Disappointment has me looking away from her. I have until the morning to try to piece this together, or I could just hand Evie back and do my next job.

I don't know why, but handing Evie over doesn't seem like the right thing to do. I never questioned my work before. But the way she begged me to save her from Igor had me wanting to hand her back so she never made me feel like I should keep her safe. Like my duty was keeping Evie away from all the other men.

"Igor will come back for you, Evie, and when he does…"

"You will hand me over."

"You are here to help me solve this case. There was never an arrangement that you don't go back." I'm saying irrelevant things, but I want to understand why she continues to think I will somehow stop her from returning to her former life. What hold does she really think she has over me?

"I know." She twirls her fingers together while looking at the ground before her gaze travels back up to me. "You just seemed different."

"I'm not," I say immediately.

"I see that now." She holds her head high.

Her words sting. They really shouldn't. They should have no effect at all. I should be telling her that she is going in the morning. I should tell her that the case has been resolved. The other girls may have been sent to their new husbands by now. Maybe that's where she's going tomorrow.

"Igor is sending someone to collect you in the morning." I say the words that need to be said.

"Am I to be sold?"

I turn away from her. "I have no idea. That isn't my area."

"Why didn't you say that? You said Igor was just checking in."

Irritation crawls along my skin, and I face Evie again. I shouldn't have to explain myself to her.

"I lied." My words rise, and she jumps slightly.

"I wouldn't have taken you for a liar, Lucca."

The space between us is gone, and I bend my frame over her. "You don't know me."

Her chest rises and falls quickly. Her blue eyes spark up, and it reminds me of a flash of lightning. "You don't know me."

I'm captured in the storm that is thrashing violently in her gaze, and when she curses and presses her lips against mine, I feel the transfer of the storm and grip the back of her neck, forcing her closer.

Her kisses are as erratic as her heartbeat, which pulses along her neck. My fingers trail down and brush the side of her large breast.

She groans into my open mouth before she breaks away, holding up her hands. This time when she looks at me, I see nothing but a rawness that's all mixed up with pain and lust.

I should leave.

I need to walk away from her, but I can't. I take the distance away and drag her back to my body, where she fits perfectly against me, and when I kiss her, she doesn't resist. The kiss is fueled with anger that has her teeth sinking into my lip. I pull away as I taste blood and stare down at her.

She's alive.

She's angry, and she isn't close to being done. She reaches up like she wants to cup my cheek. Her fingers press painfully against the wound that opens. Liquid flows down my face. Before I can ask her what the fuck she's doing, she's kissing me again. My face burns but my cock throbs harder, wanting to be inside that tight ass.

She tries to pull away again, but I don't allow it, picking her up off the floor and placing her onto the bed. She's scrambling away like she doesn't want this, but her eyes tell me a different story. Her eyes shine with a slight madness like she isn't sure what she's doing either.

As I drag her back, her hand connects with my unmarked cheek. It doesn't stop the shock of the impact. Her actions are joined with words, and I spin her around quickly while pulling up her long skirt. I keep her perfectly rounded ass in the air as I bring my hand down on her creamy skin. She screams and tries to get away. I'm not as gentle the second time, and she cries out, making my cock stir. The skin turns red instantly, and I hit the same place. The sting along my palm runs up my arm, and I give her ass a few more slaps before I release her, and she crumbles onto the bed.

Her small hands tighten into the sheets as she tries to pull herself up.

"Don't move." I run my hands over her red ass, and she tries to move away.

"You want me to spank you again?"

She remains still as I rub the raw skin. I'm tempted to place kisses over the swollen flesh, but she doesn't deserve that right now. I unbutton my trousers and push them, along with my boxers, down my hips.

Evie turns her head, her eyes on fire, and I grin at her.

"You want me to fuck your ass?"

Her cheeks grow redder. They are still damp from her falling tears, and I don't stop her as she faces me.

"No." She lies back. "Why not take me fully?" She closes her eyes, but a smile dances with madness across her bitten lips.

"I can't."

"Coward." The word from her lips has me moving over her. Her gaze meets mine.

"Be careful, printsessa," I warn her and run my fingers down her cheek. She tries to move her face away from me. My cock rests on her pussy, and I want nothing more than to drive it into her. "Don't push me."

Her smile widens. "The Handler? Hmm."

I'm ready to move away from her. She's lost her mind, taunting me. Doubt clouds her eyes, and I see that's what she's doing. She's testing me.

I grin down at her. "You think if I fuck you, I'll pay for you?" I laugh, and her face flames up.

She tries to get off the bed, confirming my suspicion. I should feel victorious, but I don't. I grab her waist and drag her back into my chest. She tries to wriggle free, but I hold her tighter.

"Be quiet, Evie," I whisper, and she stills in my arms. She's willing to give me all of her in hopes that I won't hand her over.

"I can't keep you," I growl into her ear. But for the first time, I'm allowing her to hear it. I'm allowing her to hear that if I could, I would. She's a rare beauty. She's strong, and she intrigues me.

Her breaths come out in sharp puffs of warm air. My hand rests over her pounding heart. She turns her head, trying to see my face. Tears blur her eyes.

"Whoever gets me won't be as weak as you." She pushes my arm away from her, and it falls to my side.

I get off the bed and pull up my trousers before I do something I regret. She scrambles off the bed, too, like the madness has taken over her mind.

"He won't hesitate to fuck me." She's trembling with temper and desperation.

I clench my jaw but don't move as she advances on me.

"You call yourself The Handler? All I see is a little boy doing Igor's errands."

I'm upon her before I can think straight. Her body grows slack as I push her back onto the bed and push her face down into the mattress.

I keep one hand on her head and use the other to lower my trousers and boxers. My body wraps across her back as I speak into her ear. Her face is hidden behind her hair, but it rises with each puff of terrified air that leaves her mouth.

"I'm not afraid of Igor. I'm not afraid of anyone," I bark before leaning away from her and yanking up her skirt.

She doesn't stop me, but her knuckles are white as she clings to the blankets like they will lessen this moment. I don't hesitate but place my cock at her virgin entrance. Every single muscle in her body is tense. I don't push inside her but lean in across her again. I remove the hair from her face, and she looks up at me; the whites of her eyes are so large as the fear in her continues to grow.

"I need people like Igor to keep me in line because when I do what I want, it's not very nice, Evie." I lean back and slam myself into her. Her cry fades away as I pull out and push my cock back in.

"I'm no one's errand boy," I tell her as I move faster, allowing my own need to build. Her pussy is painfully tight around my cock. The pain and pleasure have me grabbing her ass. Her cries don't stop, but she doesn't stop me either. Even if she wanted to, I wouldn't allow it.

I move faster, and her pussy clenches and releases around me. A warmth seeps from her, and I look down as I draw my cock out to see blood smeared across it.

She's no longer a virgin. There's no reason to hold back. Her cries have stopped as I grip her hips and force her to arch her ass up so I can bury myself inside her. My flesh slaps against hers, and the pleasure grows.

Her pussy clenches around my cock again, and I keep going until I feel myself ready to let go. I wait until the last second before I pull my cock out of her pussy. My cum spills down her leg and onto the bed. Blood mixes with my cum, and I stare at it as the room stops spinning and the natural sounds of the space come fully back. I can hear my heavy breathing and her cries, which are soft but filled with pain.

She tries to crawl away from me, but I grip her thighs. Her head swings around, fire burning in her blue eyes, tears staining her cheeks.

"Don't move," I order and leave her to go to the bathroom, where I clean myself and return with a cloth for her.

She hasn't moved, and I take my time cleaning her up. She flinches when I touch her pussy with the cloth. I'm gentle, but no doubt she's tender. Once she's cleaned, I pull her skirt back on.

"Now you can move." She doesn't instantly, but when she does, it's like a wounded animal.

Once she manages to get off the bed, she spins around and faces me. Folding her arms across her chest, I can see she's fighting a million emotions.

"The next time you taunt a man, be sure you're ready for the outcome." I don't want there to be a next time, and the idea of any other man putting his hands on Evie has me pulling the covers off the bed so she can't see my face.

She poked me, and I responded.

Tomorrow the doctor will examine her and see she isn't a virgin.

CHAPTER FOURTEEN

EVIE

THE AIR HAS LODGED itself in my lungs. Lucca hasn't moved, and I want nothing more than for him to leave. He's speaking. His mouth is moving, and I can read the words, but I can't hear him over the roar of my blood that races through my veins.

He snaps his fingers angrily as he advances on me. He stops a foot away from me, and I can't help when my shoulders curl forward as if they can protect me.

"You didn't stop me, so don't keep looking at me like that." His words are low but fueled with anger.

I'm numb.

I think I am until I have the thought, and my body burns with pain, humiliation, and confusion.

It wasn't what I expected. He didn't react as I thought he would. I thought if I taunted him that he would take away my virginity, the one thing that has held me in this prison. I just didn't think he would take it so viciously.

He snaps his fingers again in my face, and I take a step away from him. My back connects with the wall. Cold drips down my spine, and I feel like I'm waking up from a nightmare, only to step into one in real life.

I keep my gaze pinned on the floor. I don't want to look at him. I don't want to think of what I just allowed to happen. I focus on his shoes as he moves away from me. The door slams, and the impact rattles my bones and allows me to fall apart.

I'm heaving for air, but I don't move.

In my head, I'm trying to calm myself. This is what I wanted. I wanted out of this prison. And when they inspect me, I will be free from the chains I allowed them to wrap me in at ten years old.

Igor would know it was The Handler, and I don't think Lucca is stupid enough to deny it. So now what's the end game? What would he do? Kill me?

My legs shake, and my mind spins with the fear that I've made a mistake. I could have been given to a man I could have grown to love.

As I close my eyes, the tears start to fall. I swallow as much as I can before I move. Everything in me hurts. Moisture between my legs has me walking to the bathroom. My hands tremble as I turn on the tap. I clench them into fists to try to stop the shaking, but they continue to tremble.

This is what I wanted, I remind myself as I wash my hands.

I strip off all my clothes before turning on the shower and stepping into the spray. I hate watching the pink liquid swirl down the drain that runs from between my legs.

"It's done," I say out loud, hoping to stop the ache in my stomach. Instead of relief, all I feel is more pain. Pain that I don't want to feel.

Closing my eyes, I keep my head under the spray. I move my hands through the spray like I'm parting water in an ocean. The memory comes hard and fast as my father's bracelet catches the light of the sun; the tan on his arms always darkens in the summer months. He's a giant; he's my dad.

He's my dad, and his arms circle my waist as he lifts me out of the water. His voice is in my ear. "Got you, Evie."

I'm laughing, and I hold on to the memory, trying to remember the smell of his skin that was covered in sun lotion. Or knowing my mother was sitting on the beach watching out for us. I can't remember what she wore that day, only the large straw hat that she let me wear when I came ashore.

The smell of crisps and the taste of happiness dissolves as I open my eyes.

I finish washing and leave the shower, clinging onto my parents' faces. That's why I allowed Lucca to take me. That's why I didn't fight him. I have no other way out, but if it gives me one tiny chance to see their faces again, one tiny chance to be in my father's arms, or one tiny chance to smell my mother's Charlie perfume, then it's worth it.

I dry myself, but I'm gentle and only pat between my legs. I get redressed with a newfound strength, emboldened by the step I've taken to change my fate, for better or worse.

I don't think of the worse as I lie on top of the covers waiting for him to return. The day fades to night, and I'm left with my sore body and a longing for home that I've never felt before.

I don't get off the bed or move at all. I stay still and allow myself to go home in my head.

When the night has fully taken over, I sit up and listen. I listen for any type of noise, but the house is quiet.

The bedroom door is unlocked as I step into the darkened hall. A light at the end has me pausing. It's just like his penthouse, and my mind screams at me that it's a trap and I need to return to my room.

I make it to the end of the hall, and the stairs are right in front of me. My hand rests on the banister; the varnished wood is soft under my palm as I stare down the stairs like I can see around the corner what awaits me.

"You should be asleep, Evie."

My lids flutter closed, and a shiver ripples across my flesh. He's behind me.

"I can't sleep." My voice sounds raw like I've been crying for hours. Inside, I've cried for everything I have lost. I have to force my fingers open in order to release the banister and turn.

He's right there, all dressed in black, looking down at me with heavy eyes.

His hands are behind his back, and I wonder if he's holding something. Has he decided to get rid of me? Fear has me reaching for the banister again to keep me upright.

I nod at him, but I can't hold his eye. "I'll go to sleep now." It's a whisper as I move away from the stairs and closer to him. My heart pounds as I'm ready to pass him. A hand burns into my flesh as he grips my arm, stopping me from leaving.

He isn't speaking but staring at me. Anger flashes in his gaze as I try to pull away from his touch that some part of me still yearns for.

"What did you expect to gain by *allowing* me to take you?"

My lips twist into a snarl. I can't stop the response, and I try to walk away from him again, only to find myself pinned to the wall by a solid wall of muscle.

His erection prods into me, and my stomach clenches with want while the rest of me shrivels with fear.

"Answer me." His voice is calm.

Taunting him gave me a freedom I'd never felt before. Hitting and provoking him was better than anything I've ever felt in my life.

But right now, I feel small against the wall under him. "I don't know."

"Evie." The warning in my name has me looking up into Lucca's dark eyes.

I don't want to share my truths with him. My personal thoughts. A piece of me he has no right to. Red hot lava radiates throughout my veins, and my head swims with dizziness. I know I'm going to do something reckless. I dig my nails into the palms of my hands to calm myself.

"I'm just hoping when they find out I'm not a virgin that they will kill us both." I even manage to grin at him, but it wavers when he leans away from me. He doesn't allow me to move, but the look on his face is frightening. It's like he's impressed with my answer.

Time drags out, and it allows my fear to stretch and morph into something that steals the sound away from the space. Lucca's lip rises, and he takes another step away from me.

"That's very clever." He half laughs; it's short, but I heard it.

The smile leaves his lips. "Go to bed, Evie."

I'm moving quickly, as my heartbeat is the rhythm I walk to. I'm in his room, and once again, the air has been vacuumed from the room. I stand still and don't move until I'm steadier and take baby steps to the bed, which I sit on.

Emotionally, I can't even think anymore as I lie down and stare at the ceiling. I want to go back to my memories, but they don't come. Lucca's aftershave has left an imprint on my mind, and each time I see my parents, the image morphs into Lucca.

This happens until I steal small bubbles of time, but the smallest sound has me opening my eyes. Light pours in from the window, and it's like an hourglass has released the last grain of sand.

Time's up.

Game over.

I sit up as the door opens. Seeing Lucca in the light of day has my anger and attraction for him tying so tightly together that I can't untie them. I can't figure out what I should feel right now.

"Come downstairs." His gaze doesn't waver, and as I get off the bed, I wonder if he feels anything for what happened last night.

Lucca doesn't walk away but waits for me to leave the room first. I hate having him at my back and find myself hesitating at the top of the stairs. I grip the banister for dear life. I'm waiting for two large hands to land on my back and push me down the stairs.

The steps nearly disappear under my feet as I rush down the stairs. The moment my feet touch the floor, I glance behind me as Lucca clears the final step. His dark eyes are alight with humor, and I'm frozen to the spot as he walks past me.

"Come, Evie," he calls from the kitchen, and I glance at the front door. A shadow moves past it, dressed in black.

"Evie."

The warning in Lucca's voice has me entering the kitchen. The table is set for two. My stomach sours. I can't eat with him.

"Sit down."

I do as he says. He approaches the table with a bowl of porridge. I'm staring at the white oats.

"Isn't that an Irish breakfast?"

My head snaps up, and I hate that I told him so much about me. "I'm fine. I'm not hungry."

His jaw clenches at my answer. I love porridge. My mam made the best porridge in the world. I push the bowl away, the smell raising too many memories I had forgotten about. Lucca doesn't step away but pushes the bowl back in front of me.

"I want you to eat, Evie. You look pale."

My heart races as I glare up at him. "I don't want it."

I'm waiting for him to lose his temper and smash the bowl or force the food down my throat, but instead, he moves away from me and gets himself a bowl of porridge. He sits down and starts to eat it. He doesn't put any sugar or milk on it.

His face twists at the heavy taste, but he doesn't stop eating it. The smell continues to surround me, and my stomach grumbles. Lucca's gaze swings toward me.

"You can't eat porridge like that."

He stops eating, waiting for me to continue.

"You need milk and sugar." I drop his gaze and stare into my own bowl. "A dessert spoon of sugar and cover it with milk." I frown as pain burns my throat.

"I'll put sugar and milk on mine if you eat."

I exhale before looking up at Lucca. Is he trying to show me kindness? "No."

His jaw clenches, but he doesn't say anything as someone steps into the kitchen.

"He's here."

I glance over my shoulder at the deep voice as his security man leaves the kitchen.

When I face Lucca, he isn't looking at me. Instead, he scoops up another spoon of porridge before leaving the table.

The front door opens, and male voices travel all the way to the kitchen table. Footsteps move closer. My spine is rod straight, and I flinch when a large warm hand touches my shoulder.

"The doctor is here to assess you." Lucca's voice doesn't give anything away. I glance at him, and he removes his hand from my shoulder.

I'm in a trance as I follow Lucca to a room where a man in his sixties waits for me. I'm pausing at the door.

"Don't be nervous. It won't hurt." His smile curls back over his white false teeth. I take another look at Lucca, but he isn't watching me.

I don't know what I'm waiting for. The sky to fall around my feet? Or for Lucca to tell the doctor that this isn't necessary? Neither happens. Instead, the door closes behind me, and when I turn around, I'm alone with the doctor. The bastard left me.

"Why don't you lie down."

I turn back to the doctor, who's bent over his bag, taking out instruments to check for my innocence.

I move to the bed, wondering why I'm going along with this. I lie down.

He turns to me as he puts gloves on. His lips curl across his pearly whites again. "Don't be nervous."

My heart is ready to come out of my chest as I tug up my long skirt as he instructs.

"You'll have to remove your underwear also."

I don't know why this feels more humiliating than it ever has. We get checked regularly, so this shouldn't bother me, but it does.

"Evie." The doctor's voice has me unclenching my fists and pushing my panties down my legs. After slipping them off, I hold them as I lie back. My legs are spread, and he gives me one final smile, which is meant to be encouraging.

I close my eyes, and I'm ready to laugh when I hear his small "Oh."

The cold instrument has me stiffening. It's always been uncomfortable, but the pain from last night resurfaces, and my eyes snap open.

It takes me a moment, and I even tilt my head.

"Oh," the doctor repeats. "You're not a virgin." His words should shake me to the core, but I can't look away from Lucca as he steps right up behind the doctor, who's oblivious to him.

I'm ready to scream when Lucca's gaze clashes with mine, and at the same time, he runs the blade across the doctor's throat. Blood sprays from the doctor's throat and pours down the front of his shirt.

A siren blares, and the sound morphs into sobs that I realize are coming from me.

CHAPTER FIFTEEN

LUCCA

Her screams continue as I release the doctor, his blood pooling between her legs. Horror takes over her stunning features, but I'm listening for the footfalls of my men.

"What the…" Two words. I allow two words to leave his mouth before turning and slicing his throat. His large hands instantly go to the wound. Blood that can't be stopped pours between his fingers, and he crumbles to his knees with a look of shock that dies on his face as he gurgles for the last time.

I step over his body as the second member of staff storms into the room with his gun drawn. He's not looking at me but around me. He's looking for the threat.

It's almost too easy as I move and, in one swift movement, remove the gun from his hand before running the knife across his throat. He doesn't expect it, and the look of shock and confusion mars his face. Instead of grabbing his wound, he reaches out and clings to me as he slowly makes his way to the ground.

Evie is still screaming when Pavel enters the room. He doesn't march in with his gun drawn. He knew what would happen here. He's quick with the needle as he marks the three dead men behind the ear, just like all the security on the ship.

Cleaning the knife, I place it back into its pouch on the band of my trousers before turning fully to Evie.

I reach out my hand, and she blinks rapidly. "We have to leave."

At my words, her gaze snaps up to me, and I can see she doesn't want to, but she takes my hand, and I pull her off the blood-soaked bed. We don't have time to clean her up, and she doesn't ask any questions. Shock has silenced her as I lead her from the house and to the waiting car, where Lenny awaits. Pavel follows behind, and once he's in the driver's seat, we leave my home.

I had Anita leave last night when I decided that Evie would remain with me. I would not give her back. She's trembling beside me, and I pull her into my side. She pushes me away as she sobs, and I drag her closer.

"Don't fight me." I speak softly in her ear, and she stops struggling. Her tears dry up, and she slowly looks up at me.

"Why?" She's shaking her head in disgust.

Her pale skin has me dragging her closer to me, and with one hand, I push her head to my shoulder. She doesn't resist, but her stiff posture tells me she doesn't want to be here with me.

Why? Why did I just kill two of my own men and Igor's doctor to keep her safe? Because the thought of handing her over became too much. I tighten my hold on her, not fully understanding the want she stirs in me. Last night when I took her without remorse, I knew I couldn't let her go. I had marked her, making her mine.

"It will look like the same men who attacked the ship came to the house for you."

Evie tries to move her head, but I keep my hand on it, keeping her in place. I'm not ready for any more of her questions. This territory I have entered is new to me.

"Igor will think they have taken you." That thought has me wanting to hold her tighter, but I'm already holding her too tightly.

"What do you think he will do when he discovers you betrayed him?" Evie's angry words have me releasing her head.

She won't look at me, so I tip her head back. "I told you already, Evie"—I run my finger down her cheek—"I have no fear of Igor."

Tears refill Evie's eyes. "What are you going to do with me?"

"Are you not happy that I didn't allow the doctor to take you? Isn't this what you wanted?"

The pulse in her neck becomes visible.

Lenny is sitting on the opposite side of Evie. His gaze is focused on the headrest of the passenger seat. His tense posture annoys me. I glance back down at Evie, who's watching me.

"Isn't this why you taunted me last night?"

Color leaks slowly into her cheeks, and I like it. She's too pale right now.

"Yes." She blinks and tears fall. I pull her back into my side as Pavel continues to Nicolai's house.

We arrive, and I feel relief at seeing Nicolai waiting at the door for us. His own security team fans around the property, but I know I'm safe with him. We kept each other alive in prison.

Evie remained quiet the rest of the journey, but as she looks out the window and up at Nicolai's home, she speaks. "Where are we?" More fear fills her voice.

I don't answer her but look at Lenny. "Go ahead. Tell Nicolai to give me a moment."

Lenny gets out, and I meet Pavel's gaze in the rearview mirror. I nod at him. He turns off the ignition and gets out too, leaving Evie and me alone.

Panic takes over her features, and I have to drag her gaze back to me by holding her chin.

"You have nothing to fear."

"I know." The lie from her trembling mouth has my lips twitching.

"You have nothing to fear, Evie," I repeat, and she frowns.

I want to say more, but she's not ready to hear any more words from me. I release her chin and get out of the car. Holding the door open, she climbs out.

Nicolai is still at the door; he doesn't remark on Evie's bloody appearance. Instead, he smiles at her like we're here for dinner.

The moment I reach him, I pull him into a hug, and he laughs.

"Thanks, brother." I release him.

"Come in."

I step into his home and wait for a dazed-looking Evie to move past the threshold.

"I have a room ready for you. Mila left some of her clothes for Evie."

"Mila's not here?" I ask. I don't exactly care, but for Evie, it could have given her some comfort.

"No, she's spending the weekend with her father."

I try not to grin at his words.

"Don't start." Nicolai closes the door before leading us to our room. Clothes are lined out on the bed. Evie stands, staring at them.

"Do you want to shower?"

She exhales before turning to me. "Yeah, a shower sounds nice." Her lips still tremble. "Alone," she adds quickly. Nicolai is at the door, but he hasn't entered. I don't want to leave Evie, but maybe some time to take in what happened would ease some of her shock.

I don't tell her not to try to run. She wouldn't get past the front door in Nicolai's home.

I leave her, and I can see so many questions in Nicolai's gaze. Once we enter his lounge area, he pours us both a shot of vodka. I sit down and knock mine back before holding up the glass. He refills it, and I drink it down. I decline a third shot.

"I would ask you if she's worth it, but I understand." Nicolai sits down across from me. "I was the same with Mila."

I don't believe this is the same thing, but I don't correct Nicolai.

"I need to find The Torpedo. I need to know for certain if Igor is involved in all this."

Nicolai takes another shot of vodka, keeping the bottle beside him. "You do know that Igor is a Boyevik."

I'm sitting forward. "No, I didn't know that."

Nicolai smiles. "Yes, he's a soldier for The Brigadier."

I sit back. That isn't good. "But no one knows who The Brigadiers are."

There are two Brigadiers, and they pay tribute to the boss. No one knows who The Brigadiers are or who the boss is. That way, it keeps them safe.

Igor is only a soldier, so he runs all the special activities for The Brigadier. That means Igor knows who The Brigadier is. No wonder I never knew he's a soldier. Men would cut his throat for The Brigadier's identity.

Nicolai takes another shot of vodka.

"You want to tell me how you knew Igor was a soldier?"

Nicolai smiles again, and this time I don't think I will find out how he knows that valuable bit of information.

"You have leverage." Nicolai stands and takes the bottle of vodka with him. He slowly places the cap back on it before putting it back on the stand. "So threaten Igor. He will let Evie go when you tell him you know who he is."

Nicolai is right, and I should take this. But it isn't enough. "I don't just want Evie."

Nicolai returns to the couch. "Brother." He tilts his head. "Leave The Torpedo alone. Let sleeping dogs lie."

I give a half laugh. "When have I ever let sleeping dogs lie?" I twirl the glass in my hand. "There are six other girls I want back. Then I will let the dogs get all the fucking sleep they want."

Nicolai isn't smiling, and I don't want to end on a bad note with him.

"If you're stuck for another groomsman, Pavel looks good in a suit."

He still doesn't smile.

"I have to find him," I say, holding Nicolai's gaze.

"I haven't heard anything," Nicolai finally says.

I stand up, ready to get back to Evie. "I have Nev on the job."

Nicolai raises both eyebrows. "Impressive. How do you know him?"

"From camp." Nicolai knew how I grew up. He knew the training I had. "I better check on Evie."

Nicolai gets up too. "You want something for your face?"

"It's not that bad," I say.

He grins. "Suit yourself. Don't be a martyr."

I laugh. "Me, a martyr?"

His grin relaxes me, and I leave him so I can go check on Evie. I don't expect her to welcome me with open arms, but I also don't expect to enter an empty room.

She couldn't have gotten far. I'm ready to turn around when I hear her breathing in the room. I pause like I'm going to leave but close the door.

"I can hear you breathing." I speak to the door before turning around. She doesn't respond, and I stay where I am.

"You're afraid. Your breathing is harsh and fast. Anyone could find you, Evie. You need to slow your heart rate down. You need to relax." I take a step into the room and pause. She's to my left. There's a large white freestanding wardrobe that she must be behind. Her breathing hasn't slowed down. If anything, I think she's getting louder.

"I told you in the car you have nothing to fear."

"You hurt me." Her words come from behind the wardrobe, just like I guessed.

I shrug out of my black jacket. "You wanted me to."

She steps out, my words igniting her temper like I knew they would. "I didn't want you to hurt me."

"Then you shouldn't have provoked me." I start to unbutton my shirt.

"I don't want you to touch me again." Her lip trembles. She's showered and changed into fresh clothes. Her long dark hair is still wet around her shoulders. The navy summer dress is tight on her bust area but flows down her long legs.

She's really a beauty. I continue unbuttoning my shirt. "I won't. I never touched you without your permission," I remind her.

"I know." It's the first time her voice has sounded real since I entered the room. Her shoulders relax slightly, but not completely.

The phone in my pocket buzzes, and I take it out.

An address pops up from Nev. He's still typing.

Where The Torpedo is and the man with the tattoos.

This is why he's the best. Nev continues to type. It's his bank account details.

Wire the money in the next 2 hours, or I'll alert them you're coming.

I look up as Evie steps closer. "What are you smiling at?" She's trying to see the screen of my phone.

"Just a friend making a joke." I quickly type back. **I know you wouldn't double-cross me.**

I switch screens as I walk to the bed and wire the money to his bank from mine.

Try me.

I close the message window. He'll realize in a few minutes that he has been paid.

"I found the man who has the girls."

Evie moves around the bed so she's standing directly in front of me. I focus on taking off my shoes so I don't reach out for her.

"I thought they were with Igor?"

"Me too. But Igor was lying about having the girls."

Evie moves and sits down beside me. I don't think she's aware of what she's doing since only moments ago she looked at me with fear and disgust.

"So what happens now?"

I remove my other shoe. "Now, I'm going for a shower." I stand up and take off my shirt. I like the look that sparks in Evie's eyes. I haven't lost her completely. I'm not sure if that's what I was trying to do last night—brand her or lose her. Her words had taken me to a dark place. I'm looking down at her. Her lids flutter closed, so I can't see the attraction in her eyes. I kneel down so she can't avoid my gaze. "Then I'm going to find the girls."

Hope fills her blue eyes. She swallows a mountain of emotions. "And then?" It's a fearful whisper, and when I reach up to touch her face, she flinches away, and I let my hand drop.

"Let me find them first." I rise, and once again, I have the urge to touch her, but I keep good on my word and leave her as I shower.

I don't take long, and I'm hyperaware of Evie moving around in the bedroom. I also don't trust her to be alone for long.

Once I get out, her pacing stops.

"Will you let them go?" She appears at the bathroom door, but her flustered gaze darts around the space before she turns her back on my naked form.

I pick up a towel and start to dry. "Where would they go?"

Evie half glances at me over her shoulder before turning away again. "To their families."

Would Evie run back to hers the moment she got the chance? I let that question slip away before it takes root and develops into a poisonous thought that has me going down a dark path.

"I'm not making any promises," I finally say, but I already know what I will do. The only way to free Evie is to free all of them. If she is the only one missing, my story would never stand.

CHAPTER SIXTEEN

LUCCA

"Are you sure this is it?" Nicolai asks while pulling up across from a restaurant.

I check the message that Nev sent me. "Yeah."

Nicolai turns off the ignition. "So, how do you want to do this?"

From here, I can see the place is full of diners.

"Should we wait until it closes?" Nicolai asks while staring at the restaurant. I don't have the patience to sit here and wait.

"I'm feeling hungry," I say and get out of his car.

Nicolai curses. I'm crossing the road when he catches up with me. "Lucca, keep your head."

"I only want to talk to him."

Nicolai reaches the front door before me, and I'm waiting for him to open it, but instead, he keeps his hand on the handle.

"There are citizens in here."

I don't give a fuck about citizens, but I do care about witnesses.

"Like I said, Nicolai, I'm hungry." I slap him on the shoulder. "Stop being so serious." He drops his hand from the door, and I open it. The heat and smell of food hits me the moment I step in.

A young blonde-haired girl stands behind a podium. "Do you have a reservation?"

I smile at her as I glance around the space. It's easy to spot The Torpedo, who's dining with a man who has tattoos on his neck, just like the homeless man described.

I move past the podium. "Excuse me, sir."

I ignore the blonde's protests that follow me. The Torpedo looks up and continues to chew his food. "It's fine."

The chatter behind me stops as the blonde goes back to her station. I pull a chair from a nearby table and drag it over to The Torpedo's table. He cuts into his food like this isn't bothering him. Nicolai joins us.

"Who the fuck are you?" the guy with the tats asks.

The Torpedo continues to chew before looking up. He beckons someone over with two fingers. "Shut it down."

The Torpedo's gaze lands on me. "That's wise," I say.

"We only want to talk," Nicolai adds.

"Are you deaf? I asked who you are," The Guy yaps on.

"Who I am doesn't matter," I tell him.

He glances at The Torpedo before he starts to laugh. "Who's this fucking clown?" he asks while still laughing.

Everyone is leaving, just not quick enough to my liking.

The Torpedo continues to eat. He chews loudly, his mouth half-open as he glances from me to Nicolai and back to his plate.

The blonde waitress arrives at our table and places a napkin in front of me that holds a knife and a fork. She does the same to Nicolai. "Would you like a menu?"

"They aren't staying." The Torpedo dismisses her with a wave of his fork. Laughter beside him has me wanting to reach across the table and cut it off, but I keep still.

"Talk," The Torpedo barks, and the laughter stops as he glares at me. "Don't get shy on me now, Lucca."

I grin at him. The restaurant is nearly empty. "I want the girls."

He grins back at me. The top row of his teeth are encased in gold. "I want three girls to suck my dick at once. That doesn't mean it will happen."

I unroll the napkin, and the cutlery rattles to the table. I pick up the knife before setting it back down and addressing The Torpedo. "I don't like repeating myself."

The Torpedo lets his knife clang to his plate, but he still holds his fork. "Then don't."

"If you just tell us where they are, we will leave." Nicolai has decided to take a diplomatic stance on this. I have no intentions of leaving The Torpedo or his friend alive.

The Torpedo shakes his head. "I want you both out of my restaurant now."

The tattoo guy sits forward. "You heard him," he repeats and rises. He's a big guy, but that doesn't mean much.

Neither Nicolai nor I move. I ignore him.

"Igor isn't working alone," I say.

The tattoo guy stands up.

"Sit down, Bykd." The Torpedo's fist lands heavily on the table, rattling the glasses.

Bykd does as The Torpedo instructs, but he doesn't take his beady eyes off me, and I grin at him. "That's a good boy."

"What makes you think I have these girls?" he asks.

"Word has spread fast that you were at an auction," Nicolai says.

"Then I no longer have them." The Torpedo smiles wide, showing off his golden teeth. I'm already imagining pulling them out one by one.

"Your boy here, Bykd, was seen driving away from a warehouse downtown with the girls."

The Torpedo glances at Bykd before his gaze trails back to me. "Like I said, I don't know about any girls."

I pick up the fork and place it beside the knife on the opposite side of me. Bykd is watching me.

"Igor works for a Brigadier. So enjoy getting your balls stuffed down your throat when he finds out you fucking stole from him."

Nicolai exhales loudly as The Torpedo rises abruptly, knocking the chair out from behind him. I don't move.

"You come into my restaurant and threaten me?"

I pick up the napkin and refold it. "I'm not threatening you. I'm just giving you the facts and trying to help you out here."

"We don't give a shit about any Brigadier," Bykd pipes up, and it shows he's just a runner for the Torpedo. He has no idea who he's messing with.

The Torpedo still clutches the fork in his large hand. He strikes quickly, embedding the fork into Bykd's neck. I have no qualms with him killing the runner; he would have had to die anyway. The Torpedo pulls the fork out before plunging it into Bykd's neck again. He takes all his anger out on Bykd.

I glance at Nicolai and shrug, wondering how long this would take.

"He's dead," Nicolai snaps, and The Torpedo pulls out the fork as Bykd's dead body hits the floor.

The Torpedo is still clinging to the fork. He smiles again as he picks up his overturned chair and sets it right before he sits down with blood splatter all over his white vest. He drops the fork onto the plate and starts to wipe his bloody hands on a napkin.

"Lucca is telling the truth. Igor works for a Brigadier," Nicolai confirms.

The Torpedo drops the napkin and fixes his black suit jacket. "So Igor stole from a Brigadier?" He runs his tongue along his golden teeth.

"You stole from a Brigadier," I say.

He moves. He's fast as he grips the fork and strikes out. I'm faster. I jump back, knocking my seat to the ground. The fork that would have embedded in my neck strikes air.

Nicolai is quick as he moves too, his arm coming down on The Torpedo's wrist. I hear the bone crack as the fork clangs to the floor. I don't let the moment pass but lean in and grip The Torpedo's head, pushing it into the table.

"Tell me where the girls are."

"They've been sold." His words are growled as he tries to force his head back up, and I slam it back down onto the table. A nearby glass of liquid topples.

"What about Evie?" Was she sold? My hand presses heavier on his face.

"No." His roar is accompanied by the force of his body as he tries to get up again.

He screams in pain as Nicolai hits his broken wrist.

"Igor is keeping her."

My gaze clashes with Nicolai.

Over my dead body.

Nicolai shakes his head. "Lucca, killing Igor isn't an option."

The Torpedo tries to get up again, and I allow his head to rise before slamming it back down.

"I'm not going to kill Igor. The Brigadier will." I grin at Nicolai.

"How do you find out who he is?"

"I can find out," The Torpedo offers up, and both Nicolai and I start to laugh.

A man in his position would offer up anything to live. That isn't going to happen. "I'll tell you where the girls are."

My laughter stops. "You said they were sold."

"Yes, we have buyers, but they haven't been transferred yet."

"Why's that?"

The Torpedo falls silent. Nicolai picks up a knife and pulls up The Torpedo's damaged hand.

"I'll tell you." He's trying to pull his hand back, but Nicolai doesn't allow him.

The Torpedo's words are filled with pain as he tries to force them out. "I had instructions to find seven bodies and bring them to the warehouse where the girls are being held. Once the girls are gone, I'll place the bodies in the warehouse and burn it. That was the job. Then I had to leave an anonymous tip with you so that you would find the warehouse and all the girls' bodies. Case closed."

That's why Igor isn't selling the girls himself. No one would look to The Torpedo.

I remove my gun from the band of my trousers. "The address."

He tries to shake his head. "If I do, you'll kill me."

"The address." I cock the gun and press it to his temple.

It's a good incentive as he recites the address off.

"If they aren't there, I'll come back," I warn him.

He tries to look at me, and I see hope in his eyes. "I swear."

He isn't lying. I pull the trigger, and Nicolai curses as he moves away from the blood-splattered table.

He's ready to say something.

I put the gun back into the holder. "He had to die. You know that."

My words cut off whatever Nicolai was going to say.

"What a mess." Nicolai moves toward the back rooms. We need to destroy any footage. We have plenty of cops paid off, but that doesn't mean we need to be sloppy.

Nicolai returns and gives me a nod.

All I need to do is find out who The Brigadier is, and he will end Igor's life so I won't have to.

CHAPTER SEVENTEEN

EVIE

Hope mixed with fear swells and dies in my stomach. I'm still in the room, still pacing, still waiting. Time moves, but it's slow and painful. Each time I open the door, Pavel is there. He doesn't tell me to go back in, but I slam the door before returning to my pacing. I can't fight the surge of hope that I know is dangerous.

I stop pacing as the door opens. My heart rate climbs to a frightening height before it drops as Pavel fills the doorway.

"You can leave the room, Evie." Is that pity I hear in his voice?

"Is Lucca back?" I ask as tears brim my eyes.

"Not yet. It could be a while."

"I'll wait here." I place my hands behind my back.

His gaze shifts to the hallway before he turns to me and nods. As he reaches for the door handle, I let my hands hang at my side.

"Don't close the door." Right now, I don't want to be alone.

His lip tugs up ever so slightly, and he releases the handle before turning his back on me.

It seems like I have been waiting for an eternity before lights hit the window, and I race to it. A car pulls up at the door, and the passenger door opens. Lucca steps out, and I don't know how he knows I'm looking, but his dark gaze clashes with mine. My skin prickles before it tightens and stretches, and I take a step away from the window.

My hand automatically goes to my heart, trying to calm the heavy beat that rattles my ribs.

"He's back," I say out loud. Pavel doesn't answer, but I see the slight nod of his head. The front door closes, and I'm waiting for the sound of Lucca's shoes on the stairs.

My patience dries up as I wait, and I'm moving toward the door. I'm ready to tell Pavel to move when a shadow falls across the floor and Lucca waves Pavel off. I'm face-to-face with Lucca. My gaze is making a note of the dots of blood on his neck and the cuffs of his shirt.

He doesn't move or speak.

"Did you find them?"

"I know where they are. Tomorrow I will get them."

Tomorrow. Why not now? "They are all alive?" I ask instead.

Lucca exhales and enters the room. "Yes."

I bite my lip to stop the tremble caused by emotions that overwhelm me.

Lucca's image blurs, and I dip my head, trying to hold back the swell that's ready to overtake me.

"Lucca." His name is a whisper as I fight with myself to ask him another question. "Can I go with you tomorrow?"

He's already shaking his head.

I step closer. "Just let me see them. Let me see that they're okay."

"No." His answer is sharp as he removes his suit jacket.

"Lucca. I was going to leave them. I was trying to escape that life, and I was willing to leave them all behind." The pain of what I was capable of doing twists my stomach painfully. "I need to make it right."

"You did nothing wrong." Lucca swings around and faces me. "You were right to leave. I just wish…"

The air stalls in my chest.

Lucca reaches out to me like he's going to cup my face, but he stops himself, his hands falling to his sides. He towers over me. "I wish you had gotten away, Evie. Don't ever regret trying to save yourself." His voice has softened.

"Let me come with you. Let me see them…"

He's shaking his head again.

I ball my hands into fists. "Why?"

"I won't put you in harm's way." His words are quick and low; there is something deadly in them, and my stomach twists again.

Laughter bubbles hard and fast up my throat and pours out into the room. "Harm's way?" I say through my laughter.

"I've been kidnapped, held captive for eight years, and now what will happen to me? Am I going to a brothel or maybe to my death?" I'm caving with pure pain. "What more harm can come to me?"

What more can they take from me?

Lucca doesn't answer, and I take another step toward him. "I'm a ghost. I have nothing else for them to take." *I gave the last piece to you.*

"You can shout all you want. You aren't coming with me." His voice is calm, and I hate him for it. I hate everything about him. Powerful men are dangerous men, and I hate them.

I hate him.

My hand connects with his face, the sting on my palm is satisfying, and I reach out to hit him again, only I don't get to. His hands grip my wrists as he drags me to his chest.

"Stop it, Evie."

I try to pull away, but he doesn't release me. Silver eyes bore into mine, warning me to stop. But it's too late for that.

"Let me go." I'm not sure if I'm asking for him to release me right now or let me go home.

"If you can control your temper, I will release you."

"We aren't all as cool and collected as you," I bite back, not backing down from him. I should think about what happened between us the last time, but I know I pushed him to do it. That fear rattles around in my head.

His nostrils flare, and he releases me quickly. He doesn't step away, and the want to slap him is gone.

"Am I going back to Igor?" I keep my chin in the air.

"No."

I didn't expect that. "What's going to happen to me?"

"I don't know." This time Lucca doesn't meet my eyes.

"Just tell me. You're getting off on keeping me in the dark."

Lucca's gaze swings back to me. He's looking at me differently. He cups my face, his touch gentle, and it disarms something inside me. I don't want his touch to have such power. I lean into his hand.

"I'm keeping you." His words are low as he moves his head closer to mine. His gaze roams my face as his words sink in.

His thumb caresses my cheek. His touch reaches beyond the surface of my flesh, and my heart is like a sponge that soaks it up. My eyelids flutter closed as I allow his words to sink in.

"You are keeping me?" I open my eyes. I need to see the words on his lips, which are close to mine.

My heart starts to pound with a mixture of emotions, and I can't focus on one; there are too many.

"Yes." Silver eyes speak as loudly as his words do.

So that means no brothel. I'm not being sold. My heart doesn't sing or fly like all the butterflies I had set free. I imagined this moment differently.

I know why I'm not free. This isn't a choice.

Lucca licks his lips, and my focus zones in on the movement. "Do I have a choice?"

His lip tugs up slightly. "Would you rather go to Igor?"

My focus leaves his lips. His hand still cups my cheek. His thumb is still moving back and forth. I'm not sure if he's aware of what he's doing.

"No." It's a whisper.

"Good." His word has him moving closer, and he claims my lips. My stomach twists with fear while my heart expands with a want for Lucca I can't explain. My mouth moves against his, and his hand glides down to my neck and further until his hand grazes my breasts. I open my eyes to find him looking at me too. Our kisses slow until they halt completely.

"I can take care of you." Lucca's hands rest on my waist, his touch as heavy as chains I'm not sure I want to break.

"I can take care of myself."

He nods. "I know you can. But let me take care of you."

Conflicting emotions race through me. I'm drawn to Lucca, and being here with him is better than the alternative, but I can't release the iron-clad grip I have on hope.

I know it's a golden thread that a pair of scissors hovers over, but maybe, just maybe, I could see home again.

My eyelids flutter closed with the pain of not seeing my parents again.

"Will you let me, Evie?"

The question has me looking up at Lucca. If I say no, what would happen?

I nod, afraid my voice would betray me. Lucca smiles, and it lights up his silver eyes. My stomach tightens for a completely different reason this time. When his lips find mine, the kiss is soft and all-consuming, like a memory. I allow myself to get lost in this soft touch. This is new to me.

His long fingers flutter along my flesh, like an artist or a musician who is creating something amazing.

His touch gives me power, and I deepen the kiss. I taste the lust on his tongue, yet his movements are gentle. Even as he unbuttons my dress, he undoes one button at a time, slowly and carefully.

The cold air presses against my naked flesh as the dress falls to the floor.

Lucca steps away from me before reaching back in and picking me up. My arms instantly wrap around his neck as he carries me to the bed and places me in the center. Everything he's doing is gentle, and as I lie down, each kiss he presses to my flesh gets absorbed like light to the darkness inside me. I want to ask him what he's doing as he picks up my hand, raising my arm slightly in the air. He leaves a trail of kisses up my arm that causes all the hairs to rise. He stops at my neck and leans over me.

His silver gaze roams my face. My breaths are harsh as my heart pounds rapidly. Each touch, each kiss, feels like an apology. Lucca moves down the bed until he's in between my legs. His fingers run along the inside of my thighs, and he parts my legs.

I'm staring at him, waiting for him to remove his clothes, but he doesn't. His head dips, and I gasp as he presses a kiss against my entrance. Each kiss has me falling away from the pain and closer to the pleasure as he runs his tongue along my clit before entering me. My hands leave the quilt and sink into his thick black hair.

He presses his tongue deeper inside me, forcing my back to arch as my body sings with the pleasure pumping through me. The ache that's constantly between my legs fades the more he licks and sucks me. My mind jumps to why the ache is there, and I freeze for a moment. One of his hands touches my stomach gently, and it quiets the anger in me, and I refocus on the pleasure I'm feeling.

Lucca's tongue does all the work inside me as his fingers work on my clit. A groan slips from my lips, and I glance down. Seeing Lucca between my legs has my orgasm coming quickly. I come hard and fast and cry out as I sink my fingers deeper into his hair. My body jerks and spasms as I release myself onto Lucca's tongue. Once my body stops jerking, Lucca licks a few more times before coming up.

His chin and lips are coated with my juices, and he grins at me. I'm still struggling to breathe as he wipes his face with the edge of his shirt.

I lie back and close my eyes as my body slowly returns to some semblance of itself.

"I meant it, Evie. I can take care of you."

His gaze carries a vulnerability like he's the one lying on the bed naked with his legs sprawled. I sit up, pulling my legs closer to my body.

"I know." My answer doesn't seem to satisfy him, and he moves back to the edge of the bed and sits down.

I hold still and don't drag my legs closer to me like I want to.

His gaze bores into mine. "What is it that you want?"

I want to go home.

I don't answer him because my tongue feels too heavy in my mouth right now.

"Anything you want, I can get it for you."

"Like what?" My voice cracks, and I clear my throat. I hate how much emotion is in my voice, but Lucca seems happy with me speaking.

"Anything. Clothes, a car…"

"A car? Where would I go?"

"We could go anywhere you want." He smiles at me.

We? Meaning I can't go by myself.

The door to the bedroom opens a fraction; it's not enough to see us but enough to let Nicolai speak.

"Lucca, a moment."

Lucca gets off the bed. "Have a think about it." He tells me before leaning in and placing a kiss on my knee.

I don't look away as he leaves the room, and when the door closes, I let my chin rest on my knee as I try to picture a life here with Lucca. With the Lucca who just touched me like I was precious. For that reason, staying with Lucca doesn't seem so scary.

CHAPTER EIGHTEEN

LUCCA

"Igor is out of the office."

I close the door gently behind me as I step out into the hall—Nicolai's gaze darts to the door before returning to me.

"You know this how?" I cross my arms.

"I have eyes and ears everywhere." Nicolai steps away, and I take one final glance at the door and follow him.

"He should be busy for an hour. So it's a quick in and out." Nicolai glances at me over his shoulder and grins. "I'll come with you."

I'm not sure about that part. I stop Nicolai once we're downstairs. "You don't have to." Breaking into Igor's office would be a death sentence if we got caught.

I can't put that kind of threat around Nicolai's neck.

"I'm going with you. Who will keep the security busy?"

"I haven't thought that far ahead," I admit.

Nicolai opens a door and removes two black rucksacks. One is fired at me, and I catch it.

"I'll distract them while you go in and get what you need."

I open the bag. It's a standard go bag that most of us keep in our homes. I strip off my shirt and pull on the black jumper. I push the dark gloves into the back pocket of my suit trousers. I don't remove the money but take out the gun, knife, and earpiece that will allow Nicolai and me to communicate. He's getting ready also as I hide the gun and knife on my body.

"How will you distract them?" These men are trained to kill.

"Don't worry about that. All you need to worry about is getting in and out." Nicolai picks the bags up off the ground and pushes them back into the storage space.

Before we leave, Nicolai grabs a bottle of vodka and takes several deep drinks.

"A bit of Dutch courage?" I ask.

"Like I ever needed courage." He grins as we leave the house.

★★★

Fifteen minutes later, I'm outside the building as I pull on the dark jacket. Nicolai stays in the car. When I walk through the same double doors I did only days before, it feels like a lifetime ago.

The lobby is quiet as I make my way to the elevator. There is no security on the lobby floor; they don't need it. I take the elevator up to the top floor.

"How are you doing?" Nicolai's voice booms in my ear, and I adjust the device in my ear so he isn't as loud.

The ding of the doors has my answer dying on my lips, and I step out into Igor's lobby. His security moves toward me. I don't stop walking.

"I have a meeting with Igor."

One of them blocks my path. "Igor isn't here."

"He's en route to Sheriff's for a suit fitting." Nicolai's words echo in my ear.

"I know he isn't. He's at Sheriff's for a suit fitting and told me to meet him here."

The security man eyes me for a second before moving aside. I take a seat across from his door, and the two men return to the station at the elevator door.

I want to check my watch to see how much time has passed. Nicolai said we have an hour. It took fifteen minutes to get here, and five must have passed. If I want to search his office, I need to move soon. I could just kill both men.

"I'm on my way. Don't do anything stupid." Nicolai's voice has me fighting a grin. He knows me too well.

Fifteen seconds later, the ding of the elevator doors has the security shifting.

A tall man stumbles out, a cap dragged down over his eyes as he continues to stumble into the security.

"I need to take a piss. Where's the bathroom?" Nicolai's voice is slurred, and both security men reach for him. He's struggling against them, and I meet his gaze for a second before I get up and enter Igor's office. His drinking the vodka makes sense now, and he's close enough to the security for them to smell the alcohol on his breath.

I have less time now. Nicolai can't wrestle them for long, and when they turn and see my chair empty, they'll know I didn't leave, that I was in one of the rooms on this floor.

The minute I step into the office, I make a beeline for a chair that I pick up and push under the door handle. Once it's secured, I walk back to Igor's desk and sit down. Papers of contracts sit on his desk in a neat pile to my left. I scan them. They're jobs, but not the one I'm doing or anything that's relevant.

Turning on the computer is unfruitful, as the moment it powers up, it requests a password. I could try to guess, but I don't think that would be a wise way to spend my small amount of time, so I abandon it and pull at the top drawer. It's filled with stationery, cigars, and a cell phone.

I take out the cell phone and turn it on. I leave it sitting on the table to power up as I search the next two drawers.

A bang on the door has me grinding my teeth.

"Can't you hold them off longer?" I press my finger to my ear as I try to speak to Nicolai.

No answer, but no one bangs on the door again. Getting out of the chair, I try to pull open the filing cabinet, but it's locked. Removing the knife from my pocket, I wriggle it around in the lock. Using the palm of my hand, I slam it into the handle of the knife; the lock gives way. They aren't built very strong.

I pull open the top drawer and search the Bs. I'm looking for The Brigadier, which I know won't really be filed, but time is tight, so I start with the obvious. It's two drawers down that I find a file on me and open it.

Another loud bang on the door has me stuffing it into the band of my trousers. After closing the door of the filing cabinet, I return to the desk, where I left the phone. It's looking for a fingerprint. I power it off and put it back into the drawer.

"Can I come out?" I ask Nicolai.

No answer. I remove the chair carefully from under the door handle and listen. But there is no noise.

"Yes, come out and tell everyone what you are." Nicolai's voice is still slurred in my ear.

I open the door to an empty hall. I don't stall but get into the elevator and take it all the way down to the ground floor.

The moment I step out, the noise of Nicolai has attracted every member of staff as he fights with Igor's security. I'm surprised they haven't taken him out back and beaten him.

Nicolai spots me, and his voice grows louder. The lobby is large enough that I go unnoticed out the front door.

Getting into the car, I take out the file and start to read it. I'm expecting to find a list of jobs about me, but that's not what I'm reading. It's about my childhood. All about my father being incarcerated and how I went to Camp Cempt.

I'm flipping to the next page, which lists all my training. How the fuck did he get this information on me? The door opens, and I look up as Nicolai gets in. He starts the car and takes a glance at the papers. "Did you get what you needed?" he asks as he pulls away.

"I'm not sure." I return to the pages and continue to read my fucking life.

"He was investigating me," I say as I turn to the next page.

"Why?" Nicolai asks, running his hand through his hair. Red marks on his neck make me pause.

"It got rough?"

"Nothing I couldn't handle. Was it worth it?" Again his gaze darts to the file.

"General Obshcheye's pet." I nearly fucking laugh at that. The General didn't have pets. I was his favorite, but that didn't mean anything if I fucked up.

It's just pages and pages about me. Flipping to the next page, I find a report. "I might have something," I say to Nicolai, who keeps looking at me. It's a report about the job.

All seven bodies were found burned at number forty-two, Court Town, Industrial Estate.

"It's a report," I say to Nicolai as I read on. "It's a report by me closing the case on Evie and the girls."

Nicolai frowns at me as he slows down outside his home.

I glance down at my signature at the end of the report. "It says I found seven bodies at the warehouse where the girls are being kept."

"So he takes you off the case saying he found them but files a report saying you found them dead?"

"Why me? Why did he pick me for the job? Why investigate me?" Frustration claws at me. I should have taken the phone with me. We would have been picked up on video footage along with the security saying I had been there, but stealing the phone would have been wise.

I turn the page, and it's the final one. It's a request to retrieve the girls and bring them back safely. It's a request to Igor. Initials I can't make out are scribbled on the bottom.

"Igor was requested to get the girls."

"That just confirms what we already know. That he's a soldier, and the request must have been from The Brigadier. I rip the piece of paper out of the file and hold it up to the window to see if I can make out the initials.

"OB are the initials," I say as Nicolai parks the car and turns it off.

I drop the page. "We need to get to the warehouse, get the girls, and burn it." I tighten my grip on the file. "We need to do what the report says before he does it."

"What if he knew you would break in? What if this is a setup?"

"This is a setup." I hold up the letter again. "He picked me for a reason. He signed the report with my name for a reason."

My past intrigues him.

"General Obshcheye," I say as it all clicks into place.

"You said the initials were OB."

"Obshcheye Baluev. That's the general's name." I exhale as I place the file on my knee and grin at Nicolai. "He picked me because the general is The Brigadier, and I've always been in his favor." I laugh now as I think of how clever Igor is. "He picked me to the do the job because the general wouldn't question a report by me. He trained me. Igor found a way to steal millions from The Brigadier."

Bastard set me up.

"You're in the favor of a Brigadier." Nicolai sounds in awe. I don't blame him, but knowing who it is, is dangerous, and if the general ever finds out we know, he wouldn't hesitate to drag a knife across my throat.

"We need to burn the warehouse and get the girls."

Nicolai restarts the car without question. I glance up at the window, hoping to see Evie, but no one is there.

"She's safe." Nicolai confuses my look.

"I know." She's safe in Nicolai's house. It's a fortress.

"He'll know soon that I broke in."

"We should have the girls by then and be on our way back."

"We need a van to transport them."

I glance at Nicolai. He's picking up his cell phone. "I'll arrange it now."

I place all the information back into the file and roll it up before stuffing it inside my jacket. It's something I would have to burn. No one could ever get their hands on this information. Not about me, but most importantly about the general. That isn't knowledge that should ever be shared.

CHAPTER NINETEEN

LUCCA

The factory is blazing in the distance. The silence in the van is loud. I adjust the rearview mirror to make sure I did, in fact, place all six women in the back.

They're there—all silent.

Fear is etched into their downcast faces. Igor's number flashes up on the screen of my ringing phone as I fetch it from my pocket. Any other time, I would answer it straight away, but not right now.

He continues to ring. I keep stealing glances at the women in the back just to make sure they're actually there. I had expected them to put up a fight, but they just obeyed what Nicolai and I told them. We led them to the van, and they filed in. My gut tightens. Their obedience makes me wonder what they had suffered.

I drive back to Nicolai's and pull around the back. The women starts to shift, and I meet a pair of doe eyes in the mirror. The moment it happens, the woman looks away. She looks broken.

"Which one of you is Leah?" I ask. All heads snap up in unison at my question.

I see how they move their legs toward the woman with the doe eyes. It's like they can't help but be drawn to her.

"Me." It's a squeak.

Evie is right. She is fragile. More so than the rest.

Nicolai's car pulls up behind the van, and he jumps out before approaching my rolled-down window. From here, I have no idea what I'm doing.

"The guest house out back is empty. I'll have food and clothes brought out there if you want to get the girls settled." Nicolai is ready to walk away.

"He keeps ringing." I don't say I mean Igor, as twelve pairs of ears are no doubt glued to our conversation.

"It couldn't be the building. It's too soon. So he figured out you broke into his office."

I nod. My thoughts exactly. "I'll ring him back soon."

"What are you going to bargain with?" Nicolai asks as I push the door open and climb out.

"Nothing."

I'm ready to open the back door when Nicolai grips my arm, stopping me. "He won't stop coming for you. You know that."

"I know." We stare at each other for a few seconds, and the moment Nicolai releases me, I open the double doors of the van.

"Everybody out." There is no panic or hesitation. The women climb out and huddle together as they look around.

"This way." They follow me to the guest house. I keep waiting for one of them to break formation and take off in a sprint, but they follow me. I think now of my Evie. She wouldn't have followed so easily. I don't think so anyway.

The guest house is nearly as large as Nicolai's home. Nothing was spared with the décor.

I leave the front door open, and two women arrive shortly after us, bringing clothing and blankets. They smile at the terrified women.

"Fresh clothes." One of them holds up piles of clothing.

Four security men enter the house, and the women, who were still tense, freeze.

"You can all go outside," I say.

None of them move.

I'm ready to repeat myself when Nicolai comes in and clicks his fingers. "Outside."

They file out, and the women stare at Nicolai.

"No one is going to hurt you. You're all safe here." He's smiling like the man you might bring home to your mother. "You have my word."

I'd fucking laugh at him; only I was glad he was trying to make them relax.

"I'm going to get Evie," I say to Nic.

The doe-eyed woman takes three steps toward me. She's glancing at the other woman, who is ushering her back, but she takes another step toward me. "Did you say Evie?"

"She's been worried about you," I say.

She shakes her head like she doesn't believe me. "She's here?" Her hand goes to her heart like she's trying to keep it in her chest.

"Yes."

The other women are all staring at me like they aren't sure if I'm telling the truth. "I'll go get her."

I leave the guest house and pass the four security men who stand close to the front door.

She's lying on the bed. Her arm is thrown over her face, and for a brief moment, I think she's asleep. A part of me wants to leave her sleeping. She needs her rest.

Her arm drops from her face, and she quickly sits up on the edge of the bed. "Where have you been? You just left. I didn't know…"

Her cheeks redden, and they are the perfect shade against the rest of her creamy skin. I hold out my hand, and she stares at it in confusion before she takes it.

"I want to show you something."

"What is it?" Her voice shakes slightly.

My body rings with an excitement I haven't felt in a very long time.

We leave Nicolai's home, and Evie slows down, pulling on my arm. "It's okay, Evie." I glance at her but don't stop walking.

She doesn't believe me, and I don't blame her. She keeps walking, looking around the area. She's hesitant, but she lets me drag her along until the security team comes into view, and then she stops walking altogether.

I release her hand, but she doesn't run. Her hands hang at her side, and her pulse pounds in her neck.

"What's happening?" Her voice is a whisper, a terrified whisper.

"I found the girls. They're in the guest house." I point to the front door.

She's taking a step away from me. Her reaction isn't what I expected. "You're lying."

I don't answer, because deep down, she must know I'm not.

"They're behind that door?" She's pointing at the door now like it's a fucking beacon of hope.

"Yes. Leah is there too."

She bites her lip and frowns at me. Her eyes fill with tears, and she glances from the door of the guest house and back to me.

"If I walk through that door, I won't be ambushed and taken by Igor?"

Her fear isn't irrational, but it still irritates me. "I told you. You are staying with me."

She stares at the door again. I don't think she heard me as she starts toward it. Her steps grow faster until she reaches the door. She starts to turn the handle, but the door is pulled open.

A large pair of doe eyes take in Evie. No words are exchanged between the girls. They fall into each other's arms and fall apart. The tears they spill and the sound of their sobs have the other girls arriving at the door. I've never been more uncomfortable watching seven wailing women. The security seems to move a bit away from the door.

All of them hug Evie, and it's only now I see I did the right thing. Her happiness at this moment makes it all worthwhile.

I leave them and return to the house. Igor answers on the second ring.

"You killed my doctor. I really liked him." His voice is tense.

"I didn't. The same men that killed the security team broke into my home and killed two of my men and took Evie."

There's a silence that stretches out, and I allow it.

"Yet you got away."

"I did."

His heavy breathing into the phone shows his temper, which he's trying to keep in check.

"You broke into my office?"

"You had me investigated," I fire back.

He pauses, but it's brief. "You answer to me, boy, not the other way around."

I turn and look out the back window that spans across half of the kitchen wall. From here, I can see the guest house. The front door is closed. Evie and the women must have retreated inside.

"Who do *you* answer to, Igor?"

There's silence, and I know my question throws him. "No one." He's nervous. His confidence is wavering.

"I got to the warehouse, but I was too late. I'm sorry. It was ablaze, and I saw several bodies inside."

I change the phone to the other hand as I continue to look out the window at the guest house.

"You think you're clever?"

His question pisses me off, and I move away from the window. "You're a piece of shit, Igor. I know everything, and if you want to keep your balls in your pants and not have them relocated to your fucking throat, I'd just listen if I were you. You have the report for the fire already filled in, so file it."

I wait a beat, and when he stays silent, I regret not doing this face-to-face. How I would love to see the strain on his face as he fights to contain his pride, which is now damaged. "It's clear the men attacked my home and took Evie. I'm lucky I got away with my life. I think that will stand in your favor, that I've survived."

Igor clears his throat before he speaks. "I'll make a record of the fire and the attack. So the case is finally closed."

"Yes. The case is closed. In a funny way, you got what you asked for." He had, after all, set all of this up. It went exactly as he had planned; only the women didn't end up in his hands but mine.

He hasn't hung up, and I'm sure he wants to ask me where they are, what I intend to do with them, but he can't bring himself to ask those questions.

"Goodbye, Igor," I finally say.

I turn back to the guest house as Nicolai comes out the front door. He speaks to his men before walking back toward the house.

"You look like you need a drink," he says the moment he steps into the kitchen.

I slip the phone into my pocket. "I think the drink is for you."

Nicolai pours out two shots of vodka and walks to the window where I stand. I take the shot from him.

"I think I may be traumatized." He downs the vodka. "They sound like a bag of cats."

I grin as I drink my shot of vodka.

"I was afraid to move." The fear is real in his eyes, and I grin again.

"Thank you for everything."

Nicolai gives me a curt nod before going back and refilling his shot. He brings the bottle over to me, but I wave him off. I need to keep a clear head. Evie will be highly emotional, and I want to be there for her.

"What are you going to do with them?" Nicolai asks before drinking the shot of Vodka. He doesn't look as traumatized anymore and places the glass and bottle on the table. He drags out a chair and sits down.

"Let them go home, wherever home is for them." I glance at the house again.

"They'll need passports, new IDs, and money," Nicolai says, and I turn to him.

"Then that's what I'll do. But it will take time."

Nicolai pours himself another shot. "How long do you need the guest house?"

"A few weeks?"

He nods and drinks the vodka down. "What about Evie?" The laughter is there in his eyes. He already knows.

"She's staying with me."

His laughter rings out. "Lucca, I never thought I'd see the day."

Neither did I. I turn back to the house, wishing I could see through the walls. I want to see Evie interact with the women, but I also know she needs that time with them.

And I will give it to her.

"She wants to stay with you?"

I grin at Nicolai's question as I continue to stare out the window. "That, I'm not sure of." I glance at him now over my shoulder.

His laugh is short. "I need to shower and get the smell of gasoline off me."

He stands and reaches for the bottle of vodka. He doesn't pick it up but tilts it toward me. "I'll leave it here for you."

I wave him off. "You take it."

Both his brows rise as he swipes the bottle off the table. "Who is this new Lucca?" His voice carries a teasing note as he leaves the room with the vodka.

I'm not sure about a new Lucca, but he isn't half wrong either. Evie awakened something in me that I didn't think existed anymore.

I want to protect her.

I want to keep her safe.

I want her to be mine.

EPILOGUE

EVIE TWO MONTHS LATER

Iᴛ's ʙᴇᴇɴ ᴛᴡᴏ ᴍᴏɴᴛʜs since Lucca rescued all the girls. Having them all around me in such a different environment had been amazing. I saw each of them in a different light. We were all free, and it didn't take us long to dream big. We could do anything with our lives—well, they could. Lucca had arranged for each of them to return to their home countries. Each of them would have a fresh start, and they could do whatever they wanted.

Me, not so much. Lucca said I would stay with him. I could settle for a life with him once I keep that small bubble of hope of seeing my home again hidden.

I couldn't let it go completely, yet I knew I should. I'm alone again. Leah was the last to leave, and having the time with her made me miss her even more. We all said we would stay in touch. Each girl, before leaving, had hugged Lucca, who was so uncomfortable it added some humor to a sad situation.

Once everyone had left, we returned to Lucca's penthouse. Being here under different circumstances made me see his home differently. Everything in me is changing, but I still don't feel completely at peace. Maybe I never would.

I turn away from the sheets of glass that allow me to look down on the city.

"You're up early."

Lucca enters the living space, and my stomach tightens. My hold tightens on my mug. I don't think I'll ever get used to looking at him. He's in black, his favorite color. He's freshly showered, and when he leans in, the smell of his cologne consumes me. He places a kiss on my lips, but a kiss from Lucca is never enough. It never satisfies the want I always have for him. He moves away and goes into the kitchen space.

"I thought I should pack for our trip." I sip the coffee again while I watch him move around the kitchen, pouring himself a coffee.

"All you have to do is get dressed. Your bags are already packed."

I raise a brow, and my stomach squirms when Lucca grins at me. His perfect lips rise slightly, and I try to hide how much it affects me. When his grin turns into a smile, my efforts of hiding anything from him are destroyed.

"Are you going to tell me where we're going?" I sound like a parrot and know he won't answer.

"Go get dressed." His smile slips, and his silver gaze holds wisdom that I can't understand.

"What kind of clothes did you pack?" Maybe that would tell me where we're going.

Lucca drinks his coffee without answering.

"Fine." I hate surprises. For me, they're never a good thing, but I'm trying to rebuild a life, one that I have to accept will come with surprises that aren't bad.

I have no idea where we're going, so I dress in denim jeans and a pair of sneakers. I match it with a white T-shirt and a navy blazer. It's comfortable but smart.

"No suitcases?" I ask, staring at Lucca's empty hands.

"They're already in the car."

Lucca is quiet the whole time we're in the elevator. I know there's no point asking where we're going because he won't answer, but his silence isn't reassuring.

We step out into the lobby. All eyes are drawn to Lucca. Several of his security team are fanned out around the lobby, but they don't follow as we make our way to the car. Pavel is waiting and holds the door open for me. I'm watching him for any signs of fear or excitement, but he refuses to meet my eye. I climb in, and Lucca follows.

"Don't look so terrified," Lucca finally says as the car moves into the lane of traffic.

"Don't be so secretive," I fire back.

His grin is back on his handsome face. "You don't like surprises?"

"You know I don't." I fold my arms across my chest, drawing Lucca's gaze to that area.

"Did I ever tell you I spent time in prison?"

"Yes. That's how you meet Nicolai." I remember that, but he never expanded on why he ended up in prison. It didn't take much of a stretch to think of why.

"It was my second time in prison," Lucca starts.

"Second time? How many times were you in prison?"

"A few." Lucca smirks at me. "The second time I was in prison, I met a man. Everyone called him Big E. He was huge. I'm not sure what E was short for, but that's what we called him. He was an old-timer in his eighties, and he had already served thirty years."

"Why was he there?" Thirty years made me think it was something very serious.

"He swore he was innocent. Said it was because he had broken into a police officer's home. He didn't know it was an officer's house at the time."

"Thirty years?" I didn't exactly buy that.

"Yes."

We stop at traffic lights. Lucca stares out the window like some scene is playing out on the window of the car. "The week he was set for release, we threw him a farewell party. I don't think I'd ever seen anyone so glum."

Lucca frowns, and it's an odd look on his face. The car starts to move again.

"Maybe he was nervous about returning to society after thirty years," I say.

"After the party, he returned to his cell and hung himself."

My heart stills in my chest before it pounds. I didn't know this man, but from the look on Lucca's face, he knew him. Maybe even befriended him.

"I'm sorry, Lucca." I shift closer to him and take his hand. He looks down at our joined fingers.

"When I got out, I tracked down his family."

I squeeze our joined fingers. "They must have been heartbroken."

"He only had a brother alive. We sat and had a cup of tea, and it was then I found out why Big E was in prison. Thirty years of keeping a secret and hiding the truth is what had him taking that rope and tying it around his neck."

A coldness seeps under my skin and slowly drips into my system.

"He had broken into the officer's home. That part was true. He just hadn't told us that he had woken the family up and killed the officer's wife and two children."

Bile slowly rises up my throat. The sound of the air conditioner grows louder as the silence swallows the surrounding space.

"That's a delightful story," I murmur.

Lucca looks me in the eye. "Secrets eat away at us all, Evie."

"Do yours eat away at you?" I ask.

Lucca doesn't look away from me. He never hides, even when I can see the pain and uncertainty in his eyes.

"I've done a lot of bad things in my time."

"You've also done a lot of good," I remind him.

He doesn't blink. "One day, I'll tell you all my bad deeds."

That doesn't scare me. What scares me is him not telling me. The fact he would share all his darkness with me has me leaning in and placing a soft kiss on his lips.

Once I break the kiss, Lucca tucks me into his side. The airport comes into view not long after. I sit up as Pavel drives across the runway to a small plane. The door is open, and as we pull right up to it, the pilot comes down the steps.

"What is this?" I ask.

Lucca doesn't answer but gets out and holds the door open for me. I climb out as Pavel gets our luggage out of the boot. There are a lot of suitcases, and that has me concerned.

Lucca takes my hand as we walk to the waiting plane.

The pilot greets us, and once we enter the plane, he follows, heading to the cockpit as we take our seats. The inside is luxurious. The cream leather takes all the heat from my overheated body. It's like a cold drink on a hot day.

"You have to tell me where we're going," I plead, and Lucca laughs, a rare sound that has me smiling at him. No matter how annoyed I feel right now, I can't stop the smile.

"Get comfortable. It's a long journey."

We take off down the runway to an unknown destination. I should be excited, but it's more fear that consumes me. I know Lucca won't hurt me, but that doesn't stop all the possibilities from fluttering through my mind.

Lucca passes me a drink. I sniff the strong scent of alcohol before I quickly drink it all. Instantly, my body relaxes, and I take the second one Lucca offers me. The alcohol has me sinking deeper into the chair, my mind going back to Big E.

"That was a horrible story about Big E," I say with my eyes closed.

"It's life. He could have left and tried to right his wrongs." Lucca's cologne has my mind foggy, and I glance at him.

Right now, I wish we were back in the penthouse and in the bed. My mind jumps back to our conversation, which I should be focusing on. "He couldn't make right what he had done."

Lucca stares at me before taking a sip of his drink. "You think he can't be forgiven?"

What had Lucca done in his time with the Bratva? How many people had he killed?

I watched him kill four in my short time with him.

"It depends. If you feel remorse, maybe." But did that mean if the people who took me felt remorse that I should forgive them?

The fogginess disappears as anger reheats my blood.

I don't sound convincing at all.

After that, I allow the alcohol to silence my mind, and I drift off to sleep.

I'm moving. I smile as I snuggle closer to Lucca. "What are you doing?" Why is he carrying me? The car journey and plane ride come back, and I look up at Lucca; only, the world is black.

I try to pull the blindfold off my face, but Lucca stops me. "You fell asleep on the plane. The blindfold is so you don't know where we are."

"That terrifies me," I say, not liking having my sight taken from me. Laughter rattles Lucca's chest, and that settles me.

Nothing is going to happen. Nothing bad is going to happen, I remind myself.

I hear a car door open, and then I'm placed on the seat. Lucca slides in beside me.

"How long will I be blindfolded?" I ask.

"Not long," Lucca says as the car moves under us.

"Can I have some water?"

Silence. Moments later, a bottle touches my lips, and I drink deeply.

I'm restless for most of the journey, and when we stop, I'm ready to rip off the blindfold, but Lucca stops me.

"I need you to trust me." His words carry a weight that wraps tightly around my throat. It takes me a moment, but I nod.

He helps me out of the car and stands me on the ground. The air is cold but fresh as I take a few steps.

The wind carries a smell that has my stomach tumbling and turning as we walk—turmoil tears through me. Lucca's hand is solid in mine. I'm a pillar of sand, ready to dissolve. The ground beneath me isn't firm; it shifts and sinks under my sneakers.

Hope of all hope blossoms like a poisonous plant.

"Where are we?" I ask.

"You're nearly there, Evie." His voice is a whispered promise in my ear. My fingers dance across the blindfold, but Lucca pulls my hand away.

"Nearly there."

Cold water pours over my sneakers, filling them. Anyone else would dance away from the contact. My knees turn to jelly, and this time when I reach up and take off the blindfold, Lucca doesn't stop me. I stare out at the ocean.

Lucca's hand hasn't left mine. It's the only thing that's keeping me still.

I taste the salt on my lips. My lids flutter closed as an onslaught of pain slashes through me. It's too much.

It's not enough.

I take a step into the water, letting it brush along my ankles—the waves rock and roar in the distance.

"I'm trying to right my wrongs."

Lucca's whispered words tear a sob from deep down inside me. All that lay there was rot. I had turned myself inside out for eight years. I had dreamed of returning here, of getting a do-over, and now here I stand. My home is behind me, but I'm too afraid to look. I'm too afraid of what I will find. So I stand in the waves.

I'm ten again. I'm being turned upside down by the waves. I'm back to that moment when I'm sinking, thinking I shouldn't have left my bed.

Lucca's warm hand in mine makes me look at him. He's watching me.

He turns to me and takes my face in his hands. "Your parents are alive."

A sob pours from my trembling, salty lips.

"They know you are alive. They are waiting for you." Lucca turns toward the shore, and I follow where he's looking. In the distance, I see my parents' home, my home. It's not a mirage. This isn't a dream.

I'm home. I'm back in County Clare.

This is the moment I thought I would be running through the sand, screaming their names, but I can't move.

"Do they know?" Tears drip down my face and coat my lips.

"Yes. I told them what happened."

"Do they know your part in it?" I ask.

Lucca's hand heats my cheeks. "I told them you escaped and met me, and I helped get you out of the country."

It wasn't far from the truth.

I swallow my pain.

"You did all this?"

Lucca releases me now, getting uncomfortable with any praise. My feet sink further into the wet sand, itching to move.

"It's the least I could do." Lucca looks away.

I look back at the house and wrap my arms around my waist. The cold has seeped into my shaky bones since Lucca released my face.

"Are they in the house?"

"Yes."

I close my eyes briefly before looking at the house.

"It's been eight years."

Eight years of loss and pain.

Eight years of wondering.

The front door of my home opens, and a figure appears. I can barely see as the large man whose memory has kept me alive steps out.

"Dad." It's a whispered word filled with pain. He's moving as if the wind carried my tortured word to him.

"Dad." This time it isn't a dream. I'm turning. I'm running toward my dad. Toward everything that kept me breathing all these years.

He meets me halfway, and I'm in his arms. The smell of home pours off him, and I can't breathe because I've made it.

I'm home.

I'm really here. Sobs are pulled from the deepest part of my soul, and my dad's soon match mine. Another set of arms embrace me. The tremble of our bodies is no match for what's happening to our soul.

"My baby." My mother's cries have me trying to see her face, but she's buried her head in my neck.

Her voice is sweeter than I remember. I'm clinging to my dad, whose strong arms hold me up. We stay like that for a while. My parents release me and grip my face.

"It's really you," my mother declares before dragging me back into her arms. My dad smiles, but I see the cracks and damage swirl in his eyes. Crinkles at the side of his eyes and my mother's graying hair are true signs of the time that has passed.

My dad presses a kiss to my head. His gaze drifts behind me, and it's then I remember Lucca.

"He's the one who brought you back to us?"

I look at Lucca, who's half watching us with hooded eyes.

"Yes." I turn, but my mother's hands don't release me. "It's okay, Mam." I touch her fingers, but she doesn't release me. I'm drawn back to Lucca.

"He spoke with us on the phone." My dad is still looking at Lucca.

"Now you can meet him in person." I smile at Lucca and wave him over.

He's hesitant, but he starts to walk to us. My mother still holds me, and right now, I'm okay with that. The moment Lucca reaches us, he exhales a breath.

"Are you okay?" he asks, like my parents aren't on either side of me.

I want to cry. I want to throw myself into his arms and thank him a million times over. "I am now that we're all together."

I glance up at my dad. "This is Lucca, my boyfriend."

I don't know who's more surprised, Lucca or me. Lucca takes my dad's outstretched hand and shakes it.

"Thank you, son, for bringing her home." My dad's voice shakes like it must have a thousand times over since I've been gone.

"You're welcome." Lucca has that uncomfortable look in his gaze again.

My mother releases me and attaches herself to Lucca. She's crying, her words a jumble of thanks and pain.

"Come on, let's get Evie home." My dad has reclaimed it now. My mam releases Lucca, nodding several times.

I hold out my other hand for Lucca. "Let's go home."

He takes my hand. My mother sinks into my dad's other side, and we walk back to the house. The small candle is burning in the window just like I remember. The sight of it twists me up before uncurling itself, and I know right there and then that I am truly home.

THE SIXTH: BOOK THREE IN THE CELLS OF KALASHOV SERIES IS OUT NOW!

Start Reading Today! HERE

About The Author

When Vi Carter isn't writing contemporary & dark romance books, that feature the mafia, are filled with suspense, and take you on a fast paced ride, you can find her reading her favorite authors, baking, taking photos or watching Netflix.

Married with three children, Vi divides her time between motherhood and all the other hats she wears as an Author.

She has declared herself a coffee and chocolate addict! Do not judge.

Social Media Links for Vi Carter:

Website

Facebook Reader Group

ACKNOWLEDGEMENTS

I'm very lucky to have such amazing readers and Beta Readers. I want to thank the following people who worked with me on this book.

Editor: Sherry Schafer

Proofreader: Michele Rolfe

Blurb was written by: Tami Thomason

Beta Readers

Amanda Sheridan

Lucy Korth

Tami Thomason

9 781915 878298